THIRTY TALKS WEIRD LOVE

THIRTY TALKS WEIRD LOVE

Alessandra Narváez Varela

Cinco Puntos Press

An Imprint of Lee & Low Books Inc.

Cinco Puntos Press,
an imprint of LEE & LOW BOOKS Inc.,
95 Madison Avenue, New York, NY 10016
leeandlow.com

Edited by Lee Byrd
Cover and title page design by Zeke Peña
Typesetting by Stephanie Frescas Matias
Book production by The Kids at Our House
The text is set in Amiri

Manufactured in the United States of America by Lake Book Manufacturing

MIX
From responsible sources
FSC® C103098
www.fsc.org

10 9 8 7 6 5 4 3 2 1
First Edition

Library of Congress Cataloging-in-Publication Data

Names: Narváez Varela, Alessandra, author.
Title: Thirty talks weird love / by Alessandra Narváez Varela.
Description: Cinco Puntos Press, [2021] | Audience: Ages 13. | Audience: Grades 7-9. | Summary: In Cuidad Juárez, Mexico in 1999, where kidnapping of girls and women is common, a woman approaches thirteen-year-old Anamaria claiming to be her future self, offering advice and requesting help.
Identifiers: LCCN 2020034779
ISBN 978-1-947627-48-2 (cloth)
ISBN 978-1-947627-49-9 (paperback)
ISBN 978-1-947627-50-5 (ebook)
Subjects: CYAC: Novels in verse. | Self-acceptance--Fiction. Family life--Mexico--Fiction. | Time travel--Fiction. | Kidnapping--Fiction. | Mexico--Fiction.
Classification: LCC PZ7.5.N37 Thi 2021 | DDC [Fic]--dc23
LC record available at https://lccn.loc.gov/2020034779

Para Amanda y Carlos, mis padres: vértebras de mi espalda, sangre y músculo de mi corazón. Los adoro. Toda palabra que escribo es suya. Todo lo que soy es por ustedes.

To Amanda and Carlos, my parents: vertebrae of my back, blood and muscle of my heart. I adore you. Every word I write is yours. All I am is because of you.

Para las mujeres y niñas que hemos perdido en Ciudad Juárez: la poesía no regresa vida, la poesía no es justicia, pero ella recuerda y no nos deja olvidar. Que los benditos pasos en el paraíso que habitan sean plenos y ligeros. Que lo que hagamos en su memoria sea siempre digno de su nombre. Que pronto llegue el día que esta imperfecta, pero hermosa ciudad nuestra nunca pierda a una mujer o niña más. Hasta entonces, por favor acepten la humilde oración que es este libro.

To the women and girls we have lost in Ciudad Juárez: poetry doesn't give back life, poetry is not justice, but she remembers and doesn't let us forget. May the blessed steps you walk in the paradise you inhabit be full and light. May what we do in your memory always be worthy of your name. May the day this imperfect, yet beautiful city of ours never loses one more of you arrive soon. Until then, please accept the humble prayer that is this book.

I Wasn't Looking for Her

She found me. She knocked
on the side of the stall in
the Multicinemas restroom
where I sat staring at the strawberry stain in my underwear.
Here! she says, handing me
a lime-green Kotex wrapper. I
whisper *gracias* because
I've heard you can take a pad
from a stranger if you don't
have one. Also, the movies are
a más o menos safe public space.
Meet me at the concession stand.
You will see Blast from the Past
at least five times, she says in
a too-excited voice. I jump
out of my skin: she's following
me! It's no stretch: my home,
Ciudad Juárez, my time, 1999,
means girls disappear like water
down the drain. A random candy
date *won't* be the end of me.
I am thirteen, not a dumb kid.
My skin returns to my bones
so I flush, skip hand soap, and
slam the door on my way out.

Bunkers in Ciudad Juárez

I'm out of breath and sweaty when I plop
into the red velvet seat next to Chachita,

mi mami. She asks what's wrong. *Nada,*
estoy bien, I say, but my heart is beating

in my ears. I am not fine. I try to focus
on the movie: a man lived in a bunker

for thirty-five years because his father
thought a nuclear bomb would destroy

the U.S. *Are there bunkers in Ciudad*
Juárez? I ask Papiringo, mi papi, who

is mustache deep in popcorn. *Anamaria,*
shhh, he mumbles. I turn to Chachita.

Maybe, why? she says, drinking her diet-
Coke-and-lime mix. *We could be safer,*

less scared, I say too fast. *What?* Chachita
asks. Papiringo goes *shhh* again. I breathe

hard and squeeze their hands: Chachita's
skeleton-like fingers crack. Papiringo's

sausage fingers don't make a sound.

Us: The Aragón Sosa Family

Me: Anamaria Aragón Sosa. *Papis*: Chachita aka Amanda Sosa, and Papiringo aka Carlos Aragón. *Place*: Ciudad Juárez, Chihuahua, México, one puddle-like river away from El Paso, Texas, United States. *House*: One story, two rooms, one-and-a-half restrooms, and a tiny triangular garden where Chachita kills geraniums. *Street*: Rancho Carmona, not an actual ranch. *Pets*: The rare scorpion, the lost butterfly, and no dogs because "we don't have space." *Landmarks*: Close to the first Walmart in the city, a Multicinemas, and an uncovered sewer that overflows every May. It's February now. *Jobs*: Mis papis own El Colorín, a taquería on Adolfo López Mateos Street. This is where I am most of the time, and where I do my homework, because that's *my* job: school.

Sor 101

Name: Instituto Sor Juana Inés de la Cruz.
    AKA: Sor. Dress code: Gray jumper
down to our calves, with SJIC embroidered
    in white on the left side. Blue calcetas,
and shoes polished black as vinyl. Almost
    like nuns, but no veils or prayers. Hair:
to be tied down, not up or in pigtails like
    Britney Spears. Boys like soldiers with
classic gelled haircuts. Motto: *Honor a quien*
    honor merece, and if you want honor,
then your books should be swollen with saliva
    left when your neck proves a use-
less crane for your sleepy head. Survival:
    study, study, study. Big queso: Principal
Martinez, who cuts boys' untucked shirts
    and pulls your ear if she catches you
running in the yard. Legend: she has a necklace
    made of torn orejas and drinks
a Tarahumara tea to never die. Little quesos:
    prefects with gray skirts, gray
faces, and eyes on the backs of their heads.

Math Problems

Math = salt to my wound. For example: ten fingers = why don't I have more to add with? Long division = who needs this and why? Algebra stings too, but one of its rules made me think: 3 + 5 *or* 5 + 3 will always = 8. Will love + death *always* = Ciudad Juárez for me? I don't know, but my city is more than a simple sum, no matter the order. No matter what some people think. They ignore the beauty of steaming barbacoa burritos, and of the hands making them at dawn. They call our maquiladoras eye sores, but enjoy their peso fruit. They say our namesake is wrong because Benito Juárez was a hero, not a zero like us. His statue pointing to the city's old exit = *if you don't like us, ¡adiós!* I love my city, but even *I* want to run sometimes when I do the math.

She Finds Me Again

The little bell rings in El Colorín.
I look up from my Biology text-

book, but don't really see. Shivering
customer after shivering customer

has walked in looking for our tacos'
sizzle and warmth. Mr. Yeyé, mi tío

de cariño (fake uncle), sits at my table.
He owns the nameless coffee shop next

door, even though I once gave him
this gem of a candidate: *Yeyé's café.*

He laughed then. He smiles now
when he asks my help to roll 500

bizcochos for a wedding. I have a lot
of homework, and I haven't made it

to Sor's honor roll, but I love making balls
out of sweet dough. Chachita says, *Go, go!*

because I study "too hard." Outside, I play
an imaginary game of hopscotch to keep

warm, but a voice by the café's door stops
me cold: *I forgot all about mamaleche!*

Flesh and Bone

Long coat, black-rimmed glasses, and a grandma top-bun: it must be the body behind the voice in the Multicinemas stall. My teeth suddenly chatter, but Mr. Yeyé doesn't notice as he opens the door. A warm cloud of sweetness surrounds us. She limps on her way in.

Mr. Yeyé: Come in, miss. What can I get you?
Her: A café de olla, please. Extra milk. [Mr. Yeyé leaves to the kitchen]

Me: I know your voice. You were at the movies. In the restroom. Are you following me?
Her: No, but I need to talk to you.

Me: I don't talk to strangers. My uncle is right there.
Her: He's not your uncle-uncle.

Me: Yes, he *is*. Please go away.
Her: Will you listen to me?

Me: I don't have to listen to anything you say.
Her: Yes, you do. You need to, because...I'm you. In seventeen years.

Me: *What* are you talking about? Time travel is impossible.
Her: I thought so too. But if you let me—

Me: What? Kidnap me? I'm going to yell for help—
Her: Calm down. Look, I know you. Test me.

Me: This is crazy!
Her: Your parents' names are Carlos and Amanda.

Me: Anyone who eats at El Colorín knows that. You could be a customer.
Her: Your nicknames for them are Papiringo and Chachita.

Me: I almost live there. You could've heard me calling them that.
Her: Maybe, but—

Me: So, if you're seventeen years older than me, you're thirty?
Her: Yes, but that's not what's important.

Me: Look, thirty is old. Old is wise, so, *how* can you believe you're a time traveler?
Her: Look at my eyes.

Me: They're blue-ish. I also see zits.
Her: Please focus. My eyes are gray, like yours. Like Chachita says.

Me: So? What do you do?
Her: I'm a poet and a teacher.

Me: I'm not going to be *that* when I'm thirty.
Her: Oh, right! You're going to be a doctor and marry Brad Pitt.

Me: Brad is a dream, but medicine is a *real* job...*Thirty*.
Her: My *name* is Anamaria.

Me: Thirty, Thirty, Thirty!
Her: Ask your parents about your blueberry baby episode.

Me: What—
Mr. Yeyé: Look at the two of you—you both have the same color eyes!
¿Son primas o algo?

Me: No! But if she was, she would be one of those long-lost cousins that no one wants to find!
Thirty: I'll be back, Anamaria. Good day, Mr. Yeyé!

Machetera

Who could Thirty really be? A sour former
      El Colorín employee? What is a blue-
berry baby episode? Should I ask mis papis?
      No, they already worry too much
about me, their machetera daughter: I machete
      through life to be the best. I've been
like this *forever*. In Pre-K, I drew a hen ten times
      before the paper tore. In second grade,
before Sor, I called a girl five times in a row
      to ask, *Are you super sure that's all*
the homework we have? Now, in seventh grade,
      I machete like this: homework from 5
to 9 pm, sleep at 10 pm, wake up at 6 am to parrot-
      spit biology facts, practice my algebra,
and write as many index cards as I can to review
      for tests. *¡Dios mío!* Chachita says when
she sees me doing this. Maybe she wants God
      to stop me because she can't. But this
is who I am, no matter who or what. No matter
      her: Thirty: ragged poet, raging ghost.

Pipina 101

Her name is Delfina Lince Islas, but
she's like a cucumber: chill and green.

That's the why behind her nickname,
even though it's *pepino,* and she's green

only when her tongue plays with apple
Jolly Ranchers for too long. In fact, she

is tan-skinned, brown-eyed, with caramel
hair thick as rope. She could also be green

because her family has money, but she is
100% *not* a preppy fresa-freak flaunting

her shiny new things. Money is Monopoly
paper for her. But jokes? They're air and

gold for Pipina. That's how we met: days
after I started Sor, she whispered in class,

*What did a balloon say to another balloon
in the desert?* I ignored her. *Watch out for*

the cactussss, she said. A laugh masked
by a cough escaped my throat. She smiled.

That's how she helped me—the new girl—
relax and take her first real breath in Sor.

Margarita's 101s

Margarita Dospasos Sol gets 101s, *even* 110s, because she always goes for extra-credit questions on tests. *Study harder,* she's said to me, revealing her chin dimple: that's why Margarita is my second-best friend after Pipina. Margarita's been honor roll queen since I met her in third grade, and not a short, black, straight hair from her head goes rogue (my curls frizz and uncoil). She gets tiny zits on her morena apple cheeks during exam week (my knuckles get itchy bumps). She's a machetera, like me: that's why Margarita is my first-best friend sometimes. Her parents work several jobs to send her and her two little sisters, Cecy and Brenda, to Sor. *I'm tired of quesadillas!* she says most days at recess. She makes her own lunch. Me? If it weren't for mis papis, I'd starve!

The Honor Roll Prince

Héctor Márquez Lara comes second after
Margarita on the honor roll. He's the color

of milk until he gets a hint of pink on his
face when Principal Martinez announces

his second place the first Monday of every
month in Sor's stone yard. His gang of boys,

acne-full and dumb, give him two thumbs up
as he smiles a smug smile. He also has a club

of rich girl admirers who giggle when he does
just about anything. Their ringleader, Alexa,

is the worst. *Héctorrrrr, you're so smart,
would you tutor me?* she says. I've also

caught her staring at his bubble butt, which
made me stare too, but—wouldn't you get

in shape with an Olympic-sized pool
in your backyard? He's "old money,"

I heard Alexa say to Priscila, her girl-
minion, more than friend. *We'd be*

a match made in Mexican heaven! she
said with her honeyed telenovela voice.

Alexa Zaragoza Ordaz is a Pixie

But her wings are made of wax
paper and her shine only comes

from the Hard-Candy nail polish
she wears, ignoring Sor's rules.

Alexa was difficult to miss in Sor's
mute palette: a real güera (her hair

yellow white, not Mexican blonde
like me=a few golden streaks), tiny

and delicate. Her skin white, but
not milky like her beloved Héctor's.

She had a pink and blue glow
coming from her Cancún-blue eyes.

Then, she opened her lip-glossed
mouth (*also* against the rules):

Nice S-Mart backpack, Alicia.
I looked around. *My name is not—*

I tried to say, before she flew
away, laughing and still beautiful,

her iridescent backpack flashing
a Dillard's fifty-dollar price tag.

Thirty Meets Chachita

Thirty walks into
El Colorín, her face

like an old, proud tomato.
The limp makes her drag

her right Converse shoe
a little, but Thirty glides

toward Chachita
at the cash register.

Chachita greets her without
actually looking at her because

her hands are in her apron:
a black hole where pens

go to live. Chachita finds
her second-favorite ink gel,

looks up, and smiles her better-
than-Julia-Roberts smile before

her face turns to ash.
Before her legs give

in to the pull of gravity.
Chachita! I yell. *What*

did you do to her? I accuse
Thirty as I hold Chachita's

head on my lap. Thirty bites
her fingernails, frozen in place,

before leaving the "scene"
in a clumsy moon-walk way,

until she runs, shakily,
through the door. Seconds

feel like hours until Papiringo
says *Anamaria, let go*, and pries

Chachita out of my hands
to carry her like a limp doll

into the kitchen where the smell
of spiced meat will wake her up.

The Vent

Mi mami walks on fire and water alike, but Thirty blew her like paper to the ground. The vent, which is how I get grown-up gossip sometimes, tells me why.

Papiringo
¿Por qué te desmayaste?

                       Chachita

                       I fainted because—
                       it's difficult to explain.

Try.

                       This woman. Her eyes...

The color?

                       Yes, but it's more than the grey.
                       Do you remember when
                       Anamaria would turn blue as a
                       baby? She was so mad at the
                       world because I had to leave her
                       to work before we opened
                       El Colorín. She would even spit
                       my milk, remember?

I do.
But what about the woman?

                       After Anamaria breathed easy,
                       and looked less like a blueberry,
                       and more like a cherry,
                       her eyes were so sad and old. I'd
                       leave the room because—it was
                       my fault that she already knew
                       what it was like to lose. To—

Not get what you want?

                       Yes. And this woman, her eyes—
                       no! her whole face looks the age
                       my baby looked back then.

This woman, she felt like a dry,
missing crumb of the bread of
my heart. My guilty heart. And
I left the room again by fainting.
I left hard, fast.

The vent clears its throat.
The hairs on my arms rise like brown dandelions.

Found Newspaper Memories

No dormí. My eyelids fluttered
but didn't close dreaming of blue

babies, Thirty, and monster men
who could pull my feet and take

me. Not only girls disappear, though.
Women too. Every hair on my body

stood guard thinking about me or
Chachita being found, lying there

for the world to see. *Found.*
The word that means dead.

I learned this two years ago when
Papiringo's face was covered by

an *El Diario*-curtain as he ate his eggs.
It said: *Girl Missing from Mercado*

Cuahtémoc Found in Ditch. It showed:
her, not too much older than me, kissing

the dirt, the soles of her feet darkened
by the sun, her butt blurred. I touched

the newspaper to see if she was real.
Papiringo suddenly slapped it down

on the table, crushing his sunny-
side up yolks and barely missing

my hand. *Don't be afraid. Nothing*
will ever happen to you, Anamaria.

My job is to protect you. Always. I
live for you, he said. Papiringo,

whose birthday cards always read
just *I love you.* No frills or poetry.

Papiringo who'd rather just hug you
than to say anything when you hurt.

This is why I added the -ringo
to Papi: to give his name more

words, a ring. This is why I felt
the opposite: *be* afraid, something

could happen to you, niña. *Girl.* What,
why—who cares? Just *don't* be found.

When Mami Became Chachita

Mi mami got her nickname when I was eight. A woman in a telenovela said, *¡la chacha!* when she discovered the maid was her real mother. So when I saw mi mami scrubbing our dirty fried egg plates with Ajax, I said, *What a beautiful chacha!* Her eyes burnt like coal, and (I swear) the water boiled. She said, *Chacha is short for muchacha. Muchacha is what rude people call women who clean houses.* A whimper like a hungry perrito's escaped my chest before tears did. She kneeled to hug me: vacuum of bad words. *We have to honor them, me, anyone who does this hard work,* she said. *Look, what if you call me Cha—chis?* Her eyes warmed to amber. *¡Guácala!* I said, *What about Cha—chita?* I had heard diminutives were supposed to be loving. She rubbed her chin for a long second, then showed me her gap-toothed smile.

Days Cold Like Paletas Go By

The wind slaps El Colorín's windows with small frozen razors. The little
bell rings. Thirty's limp, clumsily clad in her long coat, is unmistakable.
I run to her, pushing her out the door.

Me: *What* do you think you're doing?
Thirty: I need to see them. [her good and bad legs shake]

Me: You don't mean mis papis.
Thirty: They're my parents too. I need to apologize. To explain.

Me: Explain what? I thought you had killed Chachita! [angry tears fall]
Thirty: Don't exaggerate. Breathe!

Me: [mocos all over my nose]
Thirty: I guess you can't right now, huh? [she laughs]

Me: When Chachita fainted, the tile could've cracked her skull!
Thirty: OK, OK. You're right. I'm sorry.

Me: Papiringo says to think before you speak so, ¡piensa...mensa!
Thirty: I do think. A lot. Especially about you.

Me: I'm *none* of your business.
Thirty: You are. And you know why.

Me: OK, pretend I believe you for a second. Less than a second. What
do you think about?
Thirty: I *know* you're not...well.

Me: I'm not the one who limps.
Thirty: OK, yes, but we're the same. Inside.

Me: Uh-*huh*. So tell me what happened. Do you want me to get a limp too?

Thirty: No! But I'm not spilling *those* beans until—

Me: *Why*? Spill them now! The frijoles. La verdad. Did you trip?

Thirty: No.

Me: Did you fall?

Thirty: No.

Me: Did you...kick yourself because you're so annoying?

Thirty: I was annoying when I was thirteen, but, no.

Me: Did you—

Thirty: You're just not ready. For now, just love *you*, ¿sí?

Me: I think you tripped, fell, *and* kicked yourself. Something is wrong with you.

Thirty: See? You're not listening.

Me: I am and...you're weird.

Thirty: Why?

Me: "Just love *you*"?

Thirty: What's weird about that?

Me: Everything! Love you, *who*? Tell. Me. Why. You. Limp.

Thirty: Tell. Me. Why. You. Can't. Be. Patient.

Me: My middle name is paciencia.

Thirty: You don't have a middle name.

Me: Lots of people don't! I just want to know *how* it happened. What else is there to know?
Thirty: Things!

Me: That's super specific...*great.*
Thirty: What's *not* great is a girl being as sad as you are.

Me: I am *not* sad! Go talk your weird love to the wind!

What Loving You Could Be

Scientists start with a question
to understand the mysteries

of life. In this case: what is "to love
you"? The next step is a hypothesis.

A guess based on what you know
or study. No school, including

Sor, covers weird talk from someone like Thirty, who swears she

comes from the future. Anyway,
my hypothesis is this: loving you

sounds like looking at yourself in
the mirror and doing any of these:

Winking and saying, *you're welcome,
world!* High-fiving yourself. Smiling.

This is what I see: gray eyes in down-
turned, sad eyelids. Long nose, more

angled down than up. Straight teeth
and thin lips. Hair, curly, but less

curly by the day as I lock rebels
with Aqua Net into a helmet-like

low ponytail I wear in and out
of Sor. So far, nothing to make

me at least smile, but...wait!
The back of my head, above

my nape, has a curve like
a perfect slide. The more

my fingers feel its shape, I get
tiny goosebumps. Stupid, but,

I *love* the back of my head.
Conclusion to this mystery:

loving *you* could mean loving
at least one part of your body.

What Loving You Is Not

I watched *Legends of the Fall*
with Chachita last year. Wild

horses thump like trumpets
to announce the return of Brad

Pitt, I mean, Tristan, to a Montana
ranch. Hidden in the stalls, the girl

watches him, biting her lip. She
was going to marry Tristan's little

brother before the barbed wire
and bullets of war took him.

Her eyes had always shown puppy,
forbidden love for Tristan. The time

will never be right but still they kiss.
They stick to each other like gum.

They prune in a thermal spring.
 But this doesn't stop brooding

Tristan from packing up. *I'll wait
for you forever,* the girl says. No sight

of Tristan. For years. Enter the wild
horses again, and Tristan framed

by green slopes. The girl has gone
and married Tristan's older brother.

The girl, looking like a pretty ghost,
says *forever was too long.* Tristan

marries, and the girl kills herself.
(Chachita said, *it's just a movie,*

but it's OK to cry, even though I
was only sniffling). Loving you

can't be *that,* right? No matter
the origami Tristan made of her

heart, no matter what she had
lost, no matter how sad she was?

Polling for Sad and Happy with Limes

Do you think I'm sad? I ask Chachita, even though, Chachita style, she's doing more than three things at once. *Am I sad like I'm not well?* I ask again, echoing Thirty. *Do you feel sick?* Chachita asks, frustrated by the third limón she's asked to slice for table five. Her fault, really: she sells her diet-Coke-and-lime mix to everyone as if it's the best thing since sliced bread. *Not like that, like, I could be happier. What is happiness, mami?* I ask. *You're not happy, mi niña?* Chachita asks, stopping her octopus-like arms. *¡Limes, please!* someone demands. *I am happy*, my heart tick-tocks an answer. *¿Segura?* Chachita asks, not moving. *Yes, sure. Now go!* I say. She goes. I grab a small lime and think of my questions as green, acid, and round.

Periodic Table

Mr. López Austin teaches science, but he
was once a dentist. That's the rumor Alexa

circulated, at least. But why would he leave?
Did he lose faith in wisdom teeth? Did his

spirit break after fishing for rotten candy?
And what about being feared by mostly

everyone? I don't know, but *this* is who
he is now: a Homer Simpson look-alike

with black glasses and the personality
of a quiet drill sergeant. *No one* expects

a pudgy, peaceful-looking man with three
hairs on his head to punish you with weekly

oral exams and crazy assignments! His
imagination for torment is limitless:

Play-Doh replicas of *all* flora and fauna
in México. Live models of the water

cycle. Ant farms and exotic plant crossings.
But his latest one takes the prize: *build a 3-D*

Periodic Table to learn about chemistry
and life. Due in a week. The second hand

of the clock matches our heartbeats.
There's also shiny foreheads, muzzled

gulps, and dreams of a normal two
weeks' notice. *C-H-O-N: Carbon,*

Hydrogen, Oxygen and Nitrogen!
Chemical elements of life, Mr. López

Austin breaks the silence, unflinching.
Who could pull this off in seven days?

Anamaneadita

The Periodic Table is beautiful, Mr. López Austin says, almost sighing. He explains the eighty-eight chemical elements stacked into boxes. If you trace your finger across rows, they get fatter. If you trace the columns, they get families, which means that a group of elements behaves the same. This reminds me of my family. Chachita writes beautiful birthday and Valentine's cards. I take after her, or used to when I wrote. But she can't build school models. Being handy is Papiringo's talent. I definitely don't take after him that way. I can't even put together the toys inside Kinder chocolate eggs. An Anamaria-built Periodic Table would be a nightmare and a bad grade, so I ask Papiringo to help. He says, with a wink, *yes, over the weekend, Anamaneadita* (little Anamaria useless hands).

Charcoal and Old Hearts

Papiringo and I are alike this way:
we let our feelings steam like meat

on heat until they turn to charcoal.
I remember I got a blue star sticker

instead of gold for the hen I drew
in Pre-K, which meant *not* perfect.

At five years old, this hurt as if I had
chewed on glass. That's when I wrote

my first poem: *I hate blue hens, the end*.
That's also when I knew I was different

from most kids. They cared about hide-
and-seek, nap time and that no one got

boogers on their food or hair. After
that I looked at them like aliens living

inside a snow globe: always close, but
always far. I still do. Is it odd to think

I was born old at heart? Chachita said
as much to Papiringo through the vent.

But no one else knows about this charcoal
I carry, untold and black, inside my chest.

Cucumber Envy

Days burn away until Thursday
comes. Chachita whistles while

she cuts cucumbers for the salad bar.
Ouch! she says, then puts her finger

in her mouth. She tries so hard to be
handy. *Do you know what your papi*

will need us to buy for your table?
she asks. I don't. In the kitchen I

find Papiringo cutting meat as if
he's cutting silk. When he builds

impossible things for me, my role
is to hand him whatever he needs.

I guess you'll need...glue? I ask him.
¡Güero de mi vida! he says to mean

Jesús (God's son), *I can't! I forgot
José* (his helper, not Jesús' mortal dad)

will be off this weekend! I can't talk,
so I run back to Chachita who's still

cutting cucumbers. I envy them: their
skin so cool. Their lives so calm.

Todo de Cartón

My hands shake when I call Pipina.
            She had forgotten about
the Periodic Table homework.
            No surprise there. Torture:
the silence in between my sighs
            and her gulping a Capri
Sun. *Wait! I'll call you back*, she
            says, hanging up. I scratch
my knuckles. Is this the first tarea
            in my life I won't turn in?
Ring! *Todo de Cartón will do it*
            for us, Pipina says. *What*
is Everything Made of Cardboard?
            I ask. *It's a shop my mom*
goes to sometimes. We can pick
            you up now before they
close! she says in a sugar rush.

Cardboard Paradise

Chachita says I shouldn't have
things made for me when I have

a papi like mine, but I beg and say
¡por favor! until she budges and gives

me a wrinkled bill from the register.
Todo de Cartón is close to El Colorín,

and once we step inside, we step
into a cardboard paradise. Table

décor, picture frames, toys, signs
made from cartón cover each

counter and wall. *Are you here
for Sor's periodic table?* A short

woman with a tall voice startles us
when she emerges from her brown

paper world. *Yes?* Pipina and I say,
fearing she is a Sor spy. *We've had*

several orders in the last few hours.
That school is so intense! she says.

Pipina and I eyeball each other:
goodbye panic, hello salvation!

Swish

The knife
that cut cucumbers

shines in
my dreams.

I tiptoe to it
scared but wanting

its swish
to open

my wrists.
The handle

is black
but glows

gold. I
touch

the sharp
teeth. I say

worry no more,
pressing the tip

to my wrists. I wake
up, breathless.

Composition Notebook

What if Todo de Cartón is a bust? I think as I see the dusty, warmer days of March erase the view from Mr. Yeyé's coffee shop. My armpits are wet. *Any* amount of heat makes me sweat. No deodorant does the job. Thirty limps inside after a few weeks of not seeing her.

Thirty: Hi, Mr. Yeyé. Hi, you. Have you thought about what I said?
Me: No. Please don't distract me anymore.

Thirty: From what? The Periodic Table thing?
Me: It's not a *thing*. It's beautiful.

Thirty: Sure. [fake coughs] The cardboard store will pull it off. ¡Relájate!
Me: Relax? You're making me dream stupid things.

Thirty: Like slicing your wrists with the cucumber knife?
Me: How—

Thirty: I'm you. I know your mind, and it was the first time we dreamt of something to—
Me: To what?

Thirty: To end our fear of failing. Our obsession with school.
Me: So what do you want me do? Quit Sor?

Thirty: Yes, exactly. You are not your grades. You are the love you give and—
Me: Receive? Ugh! Your poetry must be so corny!

Thirty: Look, just talk to Chachita and Papiringo.
Me: I talk to them all the time!

Thirty: Not about this. Once they understand you're not well, they'll get you out of Sor fast!

Me: Sor is the best school in Ciudad Juárez! Mis papis work hard to pay for it. I—

Thirty: *Like* going there? Really? That's a lie, and you know it.

Me: I *do* like it. I like competition. To be challenged. You wouldn't understand that.

Thirty: Of course I would. We're the same person!

Me: Why are you a poet and not a doctor then?

Thirty: Because—what does that have to do with anything?

Me: Everything! I don't limp. You do. I will be a doctor. You're not. So?

Thirty: I was in medical school. There. Do you believe me now?

Me: What happened?

Thirty: It was—wrong. My brain just shut down. Poetry—

Me: Maybe it was wrong for *you*.

Thirty: Would you let me finish? Poetry saved me.

Me: Sure. [I return the fake cough]

Thirty: Why did you stop writing? Are you too grown up now?

Me: Maybe, and I don't have time for that.

Thirty: I remember that excuse. That's why I bought you this. [she holds up a Composition notebook]

Me: Thank you, but no thank you. I don't do that anymore.

Thirty: [slaps the black-and-white marbled notebook on the table and walks out]

Me: Hey, take this thing with you!

Bad Poem

With eyes closed, I mumble chemical elements like a prayer. Index cards cover the table. *Take a break*, Chachita barks, startling me and swiping every card away into her apron. Rage bubbles in my cheeks until I see she's left my backpack behind. Inside, the innocent Composition waits.

C-H-O-N, chon, like
a calzón, we wear
the Carbon, Hydro-
gen, Oxygen
in our cells and soul—
(terrible)

12, 1, 16, 14:
that's how fat
their atoms are.
Átomo is the tiniest
matter you can find.
(horrible)

Carbon is in pencils
and diamonds alike.
Hydrogen and Oxygen
make up water: 2Hs
1O. Nitrogen you can
dig from cow—dung?
(gross)

Life is not a poem, life
is chemistry. Thirty's record
is scratched. Thirty's song is—
(wrong)

Cardboard Tragedy

Monday comes, and most of Sor's 7th grade
        shows up with the same Periodic
Table. The prefect at the metallic door who
        takes note of who "respects" the 8
am bell eyes us. Principal Martinez is cross
        armed and purse lipped. I feel shame
like I've never felt before: I cheated and every-
        body knows. We wait in the yard
to face Mr. López Austin. The air weighs
        like steel and rocks on my shoulders.
Margarita walks in at 7:58 am. Usually, this
        earns you a lecture from prefect or
principal (whoever is closest). Instead, we
        hear a loud *That's why you're always*
first place from the principal. Margarita
        joins me, carrying a large shoe box
with three fingers in Band-Aids. She opens
        the lid to show me the inside: empty
matchstick boxes are hot glued to house her
        chemical elements. She asks to see
mine. I gulp when she realizes it's another
        replica. *How nice to pay someone to*
do your work. I'm not sure if we should be
        friends anymore, she says. I blink.
How is this happening? Pipina startles me
        back to reality when she yells, *Saved*
by Todo de Cartón, right? blind to Margarita's
        burning eyes and skin.

Priscila Bakes a Cake

Laughing is the last thing I want to do, but even I break down when Priscila walks to the front of the class carrying what looks like another store-bought Periodic Table. Then, she opens the lid: her Periodic Table is made of cake! Blue frosting makes up the columns and rows, and black frosting spells the symbols of the elements. But that's not the funny part: the sugar has started to melt, so, when she cuts each of us a piece, it's a mess. Héctor makes it worse when he yells, *ew, a hair!* I find out her cake came from La Rosa de Oro, a chain of panaderías her family owns. She's probably rich, but her grade wasn't bought: 95. Not 80, like us, the Todo-de-Cartón cheats.

México Lindo and Impossible

I tell Pipina what Margarita said
during recess. She just offers me

a Twizzler. I fight the sweet rubber
with angry teeth and wonder about

Pipina's world, full of options. Money
does that. That's why she will never

understand me or Margarita, and why
what she said to me hurts. Good grades

don't meant anything to her. As long as
she chews sugar and draws cartoons she's

A-OK. That's what she does instead
of paying attention in class. The margins

of her notebooks are covered with eyes,
butterflies, or whatever she's daydreaming

about. I wander back to the day when
Margarita and I visited Pipina: a security

guard asked our names and wrote
Chachita's license plate down before

opening the gilded fence to her neighborhood. The bushes outside her oak and glass

door were shaped like snow cones. Her
hallway shone with Murano glass lamps.

I know this because Chachita has *México
Lindo*, a book that shows rich houses with

things too beautiful and impossible for us
to have. And yet, there I was, eating *with*

and *on* the impossible when Pipina showed
us how to use perfectly ironed monogrammed

fabric napkins to fight splashes and blots
from the heavenly chile verde sopa Laurita,

her cook, made. Margarita stared at Pipina,
her apple cheeks burgundy. *What?* Pipina

said. I dropped the spoon over the soup,
spraying my clothes with green. *You see!*

Pipina said, laughing. *Please don't teach
me manners, pobre niña rica!* Margarita

said and left. *Earth to Anamaria!* Pipina
says. I come back to the present. *Do you*

even care about Laurita? I say. *Do you
ever wonder about her life? I doubt it. You*

are just a poor little rich girl who draws!

After School in El Colorín

Homework doesn't help me forget about Pipina and Margarita. I get the Composition. I close my eyes and breathe. An image plays over and over in my head.

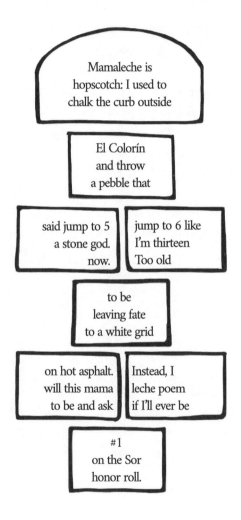

Mamaleche is
hopscotch: I used to
chalk the curb outside

El Colorín
and throw
a pebble that

said jump to 5
a stone god.
now.

jump to 6 like
I'm thirteen
Too old

to be
leaving fate
to a white grid

on hot asphalt.
will this mama
to be and ask

Instead, I
leche poem
if I'll ever be

#1
on the Sor
honor roll.

Like a Siren

The Composition calls to me. This time I don't close my eyes. I just look around.

El Colorín
is a multicolored finch.
El Colorín
is the name of mis papis' taquería.
El Colorín
is Chachita praying Padres
Nuestros, stirring salsa.
El Colorín
is Papiringo handling hot
grills like cincel
en piedra tibia.
El Colorín
is twenty wooden tables, washed
cement floors, a "lunch
rush" that goes
from 12-7.
El Colorín is my second home.

Poetry/Poesía

I wonder about the game Spanish and English play in poetry. *Cincel en piedra tibia* versus *chisel on lukewarm stone*. The sounds tickle my ears almost the same, but it *has* to be in Spanish. Why? I'm not sure. My first language is Spanish, and I've been learning English since kindergarten. Both feel right on my tongue. Can poems-poems do that? If not, *who* writes the poetry rules? Poets-poets? Who are they? Do they take calls? What do they look like? Perhaps a little or a lot like—me? I just know that without Spanish *and* English my poems would be like the Mexican flag without the águila. Like a starless U.S. flag. Like huevos sin sal. And *who* likes saltless eggs? Absolutamente *no one*!

Mean Mother = Mean Daughter?

Chachita comes over to my table/
desk when there's a dinner rush

pause. She reads my Colorín poem
and calls Papiringo over. *Guau! You*

didn't get that from me, he says.
Maybe a little from me? Chachita says,

proud. Their eyes shine more than
when they see my monthly Sor

reports. I don't know why. It's just
a poem. *¡Servicio, señora!* a woman

calls. Papiringo leaves. Chachita duck-
walks to her. Duck-walking means

that every step she takes, her toes point
completely out to make her flat feet

hurt less (she says). She just doesn't
want to spend money on special shoes.

I can't see the woman, or who she's
with, but she talks to Chachita too

loudly. I cuss under my breath.
Chachita's motto is probably on

her smiling face: *every* customer
is *always* right even if they're *not.*

When she leaves for the kitchen, I
gasp: it's Alexa in twenty years: just

as beautiful, just as mean. Teen Alexa
is hunched over, and looking at her Hard-

Candy-painted thumbs. She looks scared
or sad. Her pale gaze feels my alert one.

Mother, that girl is staring at me, Alexa
says, pretending not to know me. *Alexandra*

Anastacia, ignore her. She's just jealous!
her mom answers. Alexa smiles. *But keep*

eating the way you do, little piggy, and she
won't have anything to be jealous about,

her mom says, taking Alexa's smile,
and blue eyes, lower than the ground.

Dirt and Nail

Priscila Palacios Allende is not only
a mousy girl minion. She also steals

best friends. Priscila came to Sor
in the fifth grade, two years after I

did. When the teacher said, *introduce
yourself*, she drew breath, but only

a squeak came out. She turned colorada,
a deep red. Her frizzy copper hair frizzed

some more. Her bottle-thick glasses fogged
with shame. She then smiled, but beans or

peanut butter or both covered part of her
teeth. Everyone laughed. Priscila went

mute for the rest of the year. Since then,
she's only ever whispered into Alexa's

ear. That's why now, when her laughter
echoes off Sor's high walls during recess,

everyone stares. Alexa *isn't* funny. She's
not even by her side. It's Pipina. A week

of silence has passed between us, but
she's found new dirt to fill her nails.

Swish Swish

It goes. *Ahh!*
I go. My pillow

case is wet
with fear

when I wake
up from

a dream
where a sharp

knife pressed
against my neck

threatened
my life. I

look around
to find its

metallic stare.
I even look

under my bed.
Losing friends

can make you
dream that, right?

A Headache Called Thirty

When the crowd at El Colorín pulls like thread at my frayed nerves, I grab my Composition and go to Mr. Yeyé's. Thirty is there, dipping marranitos into café de olla. I try to hide the notebook.

Thirty: Want some?
Me: No, thank you. I don't like marranitos.

Thirty: Not *yet*. You've been writing. Would you show me?
Me: No.

Thirty: Come on! Why not?
Me: I don't want to, and—I'm not good at this.

Thirty: Says who? Show me.
Me: OK, here. [I let the Composition drop in her hands]

Thirty: [she mouths my words]
Me: So?

Thirty: So I'm happy you're writing. I was twenty-five when I started again.
Me: Why don't you just say they're bad?

Thirty: They're not, especially the mamaleche one. But poems should just *be*. That's enough.
Me: *Again* with the weird.

Thirty: Never mind. We need to talk about the girls.
Me: What girls? We're talking about my poetry!

Thirty: The girls who've been taken and found. How does that make you feel?

Me: Horrible. What else do you expect me to feel? I'm *not* a rock.

Thirty: I guess I meant, are you scared?

Me: No. Yes. I mean—

Thirty: I was scared too.

Me: You were?

Thirty: I still am. I worry about you. About every girl.

Me: I know mis papis are scared.

Thirty: Papiringo and Chachita will take care of you. Mr. Yeyé too. Do you know why?

Me: No, and I don't know what that has to do with this.

Thirty: Ask him.

Me: I will not. That's *super* weird.

Thirty: Fine. How are you doing with loving *you*?

Me: Do we have to switch from one thing to another so fast? You're giving me a headache.

Thirty: That's not me. It's not sleeping right because of the dreams.

Me: I'd say death dreams. Wait! How—

Thirty: This is the second one, Anamaria, but it could be the last if—

Me: *If* I leave Sor? Not a chance. *If* I love me and write poetry? Neither is working.

Thirty: That's because you still don't know what loving you is.

Me: So tell me! All I've come up with is what it *could* be and what it's *not.*

Thirty: That's a start. Now try *this*: give Pipina a break, Priscila a chance, and Margarita a call.

She gulps down the rest of her coffee, finishes off her marranito in one bite, and walks out.

Apology Acrostic

No break or chance, but the Margarita call? I want to. But how can I explain my Todo-de-Cartón mistake? I feel my brain boiling, until I get the Composition.

Margarita: we found
a daisy in your name during
recess, two years ago. Ms.
G, the English teacher, said,
"a smart girl, and a daisy too."
Ridiculous, we thought, but
it's true! Margarita = daisy!
Take this NOT rich girl back?
Anamaria. XOXO.

Glued Girl

We made it! Chachita screams. Made it where?
        I think, watching Chachita fizz like
a just-opened Coca-Cola bottle. She shows
        me an *El Diario* ad: *Feria Juárez 1999*
featuring El Cucuy Roller Coaster, Pancho
        Villa's Pirate Ship, Heart Attack Drop
Tower, Ferris Wheel. Special guest, one day
        only: Los voladores de Papantla—
witness their mystical flight! But we always
        go to the fair, I think. *El Colorín made*
it: we got a spot, a tiny one, but a spot is
        a spot, Chachita says, buzzing like
a gnat. *Oh,* I say, disappointed, because I
        will be glued to this "spot." *Hija,*
this means money, publicity. Smile! Chachita
        begs. I give her a Mona Lisa smile.
You'll still be able to go on the Ferris Wheel!
        She laughs. I don't. I've been scared of
that moving piece of metal since I had to yell
        to let me down when I was little. *What*
about The Papantla fliers? You've never seen
        them! Chachita says. True, I've only heard
of them, but am I supposed to see them with
        binoculars from wherever this spot is?
I go to my room. Being a girl in Ciudad Juárez
        sucks: I can *never* go anywhere alone.

My Feria Plan

It takes me a week,
but it's gold: 1. Invite

Margarita (if she takes
me back) 2. Hold hands (like

little girls, ugh) 3. Buy
whistles and pepper spray

(a woman must, I read
somewhere) 4. Talk

to no one (except
each other) 5. Look

at no one (except for
the voladores).

It takes exacly one
minute for Chachita

and Papiringo to say *no!*
give no explanation, and

pay no compliments
to their friendless,

machetera daughter
on her genius plan.

Escaping Mini El Colorín

The smoke coming off the grill in El Colorín's spot at the fair is thick and black. I cough in my assigned corner, eating tostadas. Chachita baptizes this hot tent Mini El Colorín. She even had t-shirts made: tie-dyed, scratchy, with a bird that is not a finch on the back. So much for the publicity of the "best tacos in Juárez" (inscribed on the front in ugly font). But the line of people waiting for food never goes down below ten, so ugly t-shirts or not, we're a success. *Want some puerco adobado taquitos?* Papiringo asks, his balding head shiny. I sulk, coughing, shake my head no. *Want to get out of here?* Mr. Yeyé asks, startling me. *Surprise,* Chachita says. I'm already on my feet, dusting off any chip bits from my lap. *Don't let go of his hand!* she says, already an echo.

Papantla Voladores Interrupted

We ride Pancho Villa's ship twice
and buy chilindrinas: a flat, puffed

flour bed with cabbage, pork ringlets,
cucumbers and Valentina sauce. We

see the long wooden pole before we see
the Papantla voladores: they climb, calm,

in synch, then one volador plays the flute
to harmonize the others' flight. Only rope

holds their waists to the pole. Only courage
and pride can make them risk life like this.

I think of the honor roll and how I
must climb to be up there with them—

Margarita and Héctor. I want to fly.
The eyes of a strange man disconnect

me from any flying. He smiles. I look
around. It's me he's looking at. I squeeze

Mr. Yeyé's hand. *Can we go?* I ask. Fear,
I've felt it before from *El Diario's* ink.

Not from a face just feet away from me.

Swish and Run

This time
the death

dream
is the man

at the fair
with a knife

to my neck.
Swish, it goes,

and I run,
bloody,

while
the Papantla

voladores
chant *corre*

niña, run.
When I wake

up, my pajama
top and pillow

case puddle
with sweat.

Zipped Girl

I zip it about my swishing dreams.
Chachita and Papiringo are scared

for me as it is. *El Diario* sits alone,
open, on our kitchen table where

Papiringo was reading it before he
had to take off to open El Colorín.

No girl is on the front page this time,
but it takes only a few pages to find

news about the latest "femicide victim
in Ciudad Juárez." I don't know what

"femicide" means, but it sounds a lot
like "homicide," which means murder.

Don't read that! Chachita snaps. *What
is "femicide"?* I ask. *It's when a girl*

*or woman...dies. Don't worry about
that,* she says, touching my cheek. *I*

think you mean killed. *And I'm a girl.
I have to worry, right?* I yell, swatting

her hand off my hot face like a fly.

Found Niece

When we get to El Colorín, I run to Mr. Yeyé's coffee shop. His back greets me when I walk inside. I knock on his glass counter to say hello and ask for a marranito. Maybe Thirty is right about the gingerbread pig-shaped bread. *Mr. Yeyé, why do you love me?* I ask, biting the snout off the pig. He says because I'm grrrreat, like Tony the Tiger. I smile small, used to him saying that. *I'm serious, we're not even family,* I say, chewing the surprisingly delicious snout. Mr. Yeyé melts into a chair, boneless. I stop eating and go to him. *Mi sobrina,* he says, lost in a place I hadn't seen before on his face. After a heavy minute, he says I remind him of his niece, who disappeared when she was eighteen. She was found dead years ago. *I'm so sorry, Mr. Yeyé,* I say, the sweet taste of the marranito gone.

Papiringo Talks Boys

Back in El Colorín, I find Papiringo
        marinating pork in adobo sauce.
Can I help you? I say, even though I
        only help in the dining room.
What is it? he asks, furrowing his brow.
        Mr. Yeyé's niece. All the dead
girls and women in Ciudad Juárez. Why
        does this happen? I say looking
at him. Papiringo sighs and rubs his red
        bald head. *I...I don't know. I...*
can I say something else? Boys. Men.
        We are not all good. We are
not all bad. But you have to be care-
        ful before you love one. Know
him well. Let me know him too, he says,
        his face sweaty. *¿Papi?* I say.
I smell his fear like I do the raw pork.
        Gracias. For trying to talk to me
about this, I say, hugging his round,
        aproned belly. His guts gurgle.

I Pray a Poem

Jesús—
You are
like Thirty.
I believe
and don't
believe in
you. No matter the rare times mis papis drag me
to church. But I know of your sacred heart because
of the ornaments they sell in Mercado Cuauhtémoc.

Jesús —
I want
to break
the ice:
your dad's name spelled backwards is dog. Now, if you
are as real as the "güero" Papiringo prays to, as in the movies where
you save the world, couldn't you have saved the dead girls, or at least
Mr. Yeyé's niece? If not, could I call on her—la Virgen de Guadalupe?
Chachita says she's the mother of all México (I thought it was a
Tarahumara or Azteca woman, but Chachita says history is not
the same as faith). I've heard Chachita pray to her and you.
She says I could too if I stop thinking so much. But I
can't. That's not who I am, so: God—Virgen—
Take this poem instead. Save
all of us girls. Save
Ciudad Juárez.

Home

"Ciudad Juárez es
la frontera más fabulosa
y bella del mundo," Juan
Gabriel, our sweet prince
of sung border love, sings.
I feel his words in my bones.
Despite all the death,
fear and potholes, I
see my city as a her, as
a second mami: black
braids cover her brown
head ten times. Wrinkles
like flowers bloom from
her desert and cement eyes.
Her heart is carved with
cacti nests where we,
Juarenses, eat from
the prickly pears she
grows like breasts. I
never could spit her
milk because she feeds
me every day, because
she's my beloved home.

Robot Dad = Mean Girl?

*Cacti? Breasts? Milk? Ew! What
kind of poem is this?* Alexa pulls

my Composition up by the page,
ripping part of it. I'm surprised

she knows what a poem is. She's back
in El Colorín, but this time with what

looks like her dad. *Do you need some
tostadas and salsa?* I ask, thinking

she's a customer here, and she's *always*
right, even if she's not. *No! Last time I*

ate salsa here, I got diarrhea! she yells
so every person hears. *Alexa. Working*

here. Silence, a man, staring at papers
on the table, says. *My poor daddy!*

*He runs a lot of maquiladoras.
That's a real job, not this,* Alexa

says, looking at our taquería as if
it was a roach. My manners go out

the window then. *Oh yeah? At least
my mami doesn't hate me,* I say so

loud, every one there, except her dad,
looks at us. *Daddy, the girl is bothering*

me. Do something! Alexa says, pulling
on his suit. *I said. Working here. Silence.*

Eat your food when it gets here, her dad
replies. Alexa turns beet-red. She takes

my Composition notebook and throws
it in the trash can by the salsa bar.

I see every color of the rainbow
in my eyes, and I feel something

like the Hulk coming out of my teen
body. I curl my fists so hard my nails

hurt my palms. *Anamaria, ¿qué está
pasando aquí?* Chachita asks, touching

my shoulder. *What's happening here,
señora, is that your daughter is bothering*

me and my daddy, Alexa says. *Is that true,
hija?* Chachita asks, looking at me. I shake

her hand off me and run to Mr. Yeyé's,
forgetting to save my Composition from

its salsa-and-vegetable-soaked destiny.

Thirty Tries to Talk Boys

Mr. Yeyé asks me what's wrong when I slam his door against the wall on my way in. I go to him and hug him, drenching his denim apron with my tears. Someone enters the coffee shop.

Thirty: Looking for this?
Me: Le—me a—!

Thirty: Give Mr. Yeyé a rest. Come talk to me.
Me: [I free my face from Mr. Yeyé's apron] Leave me alone, I said.

Thirty: And *I* said, looking for *this*?
Me: What!

Thirty: [she holds my Composition up]
Me: [I run to get it—it's not soiled at all!]

Thirty: I saw the whole thing from a corner table.
Me: Thank you, thank you!

Thirty: What happened? I don't remember Alexa being that bad.
Me: I don't care what you remember. She's mean!

Thirty: You weren't exactly kind to her, either.
Me: I tried, but she's...evil!

Thirty: Whoa! She's not evil. She's just sad.
Me: What, sad like me?

Thirty: Maybe. I don't know her too much, but I saw her dad—
Me: Why are you defending her?

Thirty: Because "mean" girls act out for a reason. Most of the time, anyway.

Me: So, I'm supposed to become her friend now?

Thirty: Maybe. I never tried. I just saw what she was on the outside.

Me: I know she's pretty, boys like her, but so what? She's still ev—

Thirty: You're pretty too! Let those curls be free. Too much Aqua Net! Do you *like* someone?

Me: What? No!

Thirty: Are you sure?

Me: Yes! I don't have time for that!

Thirty: But you have time for Brad Pitt who you only see in movies?

Me: I told you that's different. Also, movies are all I do for fun, and he's—he's—

Thirty: Gorgeous?

Me: Yes. Everyone knows that.

Thirty: Can I tell you about my "Brad Pitt"?

Me: No, thank you. What for?

Thirty: Because…it's fun! Come on!

Me: OK, OK.

Thirty: He has the most beautiful azabache hair. His eyes are brown and sleepy. His name is—

Me: Sorry, no. Can't.

Thirty: Don't you care about *real* love? At least ask Chachita and Papiringo how they met!

Me: ¡Adiós!

Jet-Black

I look up "azabache": it's the before-
coal. A gemstone. Does Thirty's novio
have hair that shines black? Is he like
Prince Eric (as in Ariel)? What
would it be like to love a real boy?
I love Brad Pitt whether he's heart-
breaking Tristan or pouting vampire
Louie. I love him because of his
button nose and long hair. I love
Brad Pitt because I've heard him say
in my dreams, Horse ride with me,
let's snack on pancakes and kiss.
But kisses—why?! The insides of
my lips are like eels. Tongues
are grainy and gross sometimes.
Loving real boys with jet-black
hair is a mystery I don't want—

Chachita Talks Papiringo

Is this a new one? Chachita asks, corralling
        me in my room. I cover my poem.
She sits on my bed. *I know talking about*
        the girls who've died is important,
but you're my baby girl. Can you understand
        I want to protect you from that?
she asks. *No. And it's girls and women, so*
        we're both in danger. Why shouldn't
we talk? I say. She looks out my window.
        You're right, but it's not easy. Bad
things will keep happening. I just want you
        to be a child for as long as you can,
Chachita says. I sigh, defeated. *How did*
        you and Papiringo meet? Can you
at least tell me that? I ask. The moonlight
        shows me Chachita's blushing face.
I met him in school when people called him
        El Canario. He had a full head of
golden hair then, and he had sooo many girl-
        friends before me. Has he told you
about that? she says. She tells me her love
        story until my eyes shake with Zzzs.

El Canario

That was Papiringo's nick-
name because he only had
to put a strand of his hair
behind his ear and say two
nice words to make women
swoon. That was his only
song. As a dad, he sings
like this: he solves my math
problems without ruffling
a feather, without a huffing
and puffing tune. His music
comes from pecking food like
seeds: esponjas, hot wings,
tripitas (beef guts), peanuts.
To hear his papi song you
cup your hands to his heart:
the beat is a whisper, the love,
a shout. Sometimes you just
have to ask: sing, sing louder
¡por favor, Carlos Aragón!

Rock Girl

¿Qué es eso? Pipina asks, hovering
and interrupting my lonely lunch

at Sor. *Nothing*, I reply, making
my canario poem wince at hearing

that it is nothing. *I miss you, can we
be friends again?* she asks. I haven't

apologized since I called her poor little
rich girl, which makes it easier *and*

harder to try now. *I miss you too,
but I have to focus more on school,*

*and you have Priscila now, don't
you?* I say. Pipina's brown eyes

melt. My gray eyes harden. *Priscila,
you, and I could be friends, and Sor*

*and its stupid honor roll is not every-
thing!* Pipina says, echoing Thirty.

*We're just different. You will never,
ever understand, Pipina,* I say, like

the rock I told Thirty I was not when
she spoke about the girls we have lost.

Tic Tic

I wake up. *Tic tic.* The noise is coming from my window. I think about the man from the fair finding me even though it doesn't make sense. I look around my room for a weapon. Nothing. The closest thing would be my alarm clock. *Tic tic.* I start to run.

Thirty: Hey, stop! [her voice muffled by the glass]
Me: Shh!

Thirty: Open the window. Quick! I have to talk to you.
Me: Now? What's wrong with you?

Thirty: I *will* knock on the door.
Me: Fine! [I open the window]

Thirty: I have to help her. Not only you. That must really be why I'm here.
Me: Her who?

Thirty: Never mind. You just won't see me as often.
Me: Why?

Thirty: Because I'll be out. Standing watch.
Me: For what?

Thirty: For—I'm not sure. But I'll be back. Is everything alright with you?
Me: Y-yes, though—

Thirty: Good! I don't want to wake anyone up. I have to go.
Me: Wake up anyone else but *me*, I guess. Where are you going?

Thirty runs into the shadows of Rancho Carmona street.

A Paper Plane Carries a Yes

Mr. López Austin is writing *DNA:*
The Blueprint of Life on the board,

which means our Periodic Tables
will accumulate dust for a while.

A paper plane lands onto the runway
of my Sor desk. I undo its wings as

quietly as I can. There's a *yes* inside
a daisy, like my apology! Margarita

has taken me back! I look for her.
She smiles. She motions me to fly

the plane back to her. I do, scared
Mr. López Austin will catch us.

She's writing so fast on the paper,
I wonder what it's about. When I

get the winged message, I want
to jump: *My house, Saturday?*

I give her a thumbs-up from afar.
That's when I notice Héctor's face

become strawberry milk. He watches
Margarita writing. Is milky boy in love?

Margarita's Test

Papiringo will drive me to Margarita's house because he's a human compass besides a canary. He doesn't need maps or directions. That's why, a few seconds after reading Margarita's address, he says, *We'll leave by 10 am tomorrow, on the dot.* It sounds too early for a Saturday morning, and it's only a girls' get-together, but I know better than going against his favorite saying: *Camarón que se duerme se lo lleva la corriente.* It's like the early bird who gets the worm but with a sleeping shrimp, though I doubt being on time worries them. Saturday comes. The half-asleep bird-shrimp in me wakes up when I think, what if this isn't *only* a get-together? Could it be a test to see if I'm more than a cheat? What does one wear to her trial? I settle on jeans and my Ricky Martin t-shirt.

Super Trout

Margarita's house is all cinder
blocks and naked caulk. Papiringo

checks his rearview mirror, the engine
idling. *Anamaria, in Ciudad Juárez,*

like other cities, you have to be careful
everywhere, but in this neighborhood

you have to be super vigilant, súper
trucha, he says. I laugh. *Hija, I'm*

serious. You don't leave her parents'
sight. You don't go outside. Understand?

he commands. *Sí, papi, I understand.*
I'll be a super trout! He doesn't even

smile because he's moving his neck
like the Exorcist girl to look at every

mirror in the car. *I'll be back at 3 pm.*
On the dot. I love you, he says, pecking

me on the forehead. Her mom waves
at us from the door. Margarita opens

the metal flower fence that cages her house.
Anamaria, come in! she calls out, and shows

me something I rarely see on her Sor
face: happy teeth. Her chin dimple looks

deeper, almost alive. *I've been working
on dance steps for Fey's "Popocatépetl,"*

*but maybe we can do one for "Livin'
La Vida Loca,"* she says, pointing

to my t-shirt. *Let's go, then,* I say.
There was never a Margarita test.

Margarita's Equilibrio

Na-na-boom-boom, Popocatépetl, Fey sings
            for the tenth time before I feign
a fainting scene on Margarita's bed. She laughs
            so hard, she snorts. I stare at her
full, flushed cheeks and wonder how she
            does it: always be the honor roll
queen and still be happy. What's the secret
            to her equilibrio? Her balance.
A knock stops any inquiry. Margarita fans
            herself before opening up. A tiny
voice joins the sweaty air, *Can we play too?*
            ¡Sí, claro! Margarita says. Two
little girls in swimsuits come in. *This is*
            Cecy and Brenda. They were littler
when you met them, Margarita says. *I'm not*
            little, Brenda, the youngest one,
says. *Oh, really?* Margarita says, before
            shaking her arms like a washing
machine. Her screams are Milky Ways:
            a nougat and chocolate dream you
eat until your belly hurts. Cecy looks at me
            with eyes twice the size of a deer's.
Do you want to draw? she asks. I smile.
            She takes me to her big sister's make-
shift desk (plywood on top of the same
            cinder blocks that make her house).
This must be Margarita's secret to balance:
            two little girls asking to play.

Once a Cheater

Margarita's eyelids don't fully close
when she sleeps. A slit of sclera,

the white in Margarita's eyes,
announces itself when I turn to face

her breath: Pollo Loco and beans.
After dancing and playing for hours,

we decided to nap. Margarita wakes
up and whispers, *do you like-like*

a boy? I shake my head. Boy talk
is not my thing, but it's girl code

to ask her back. She surprises me
when she uses "Héctor" as subject,

verb and object. *What does boy*
love feel like? I ask. I actually

want to know. Margarita stares
at the neon stars and Backstreet

Boys poster on the ceiling for
so long I feel I might turn thirty

before she tells me she feels like
a blind moth when he's near.

It's the most wonderful thing, she
concludes, absolute and wise.

*Don't you think that he's a little
bit too spoiled?* I ask. *Maybe, but*

*what does that have to do with any-
thing?* she replies. *He's rich, you're*

*not, he wouldn't understand you,
just like you said Pipina couldn't*

understand us, I say. Margarita
stands up, arrow-like. *I never said*

*that, and anyway, this is different!
He calls me. He says he likes me.*

*Not my house or neighborhood!
Plus, I'm working hard to be*

*someone. He understands that,
unlike you, cheater,* Margarita says.

Oh, look at that, it's almost 3, bye!
she adds. Her sisters' second knock

fills me with something unnamable.
Can we play? Cecy and Brenda ask.

Gasp

I wake up,
my armpits

soup. I
didn't see

a knife or
a man

this time.
I just felt

my heart
leap out

of my chest.
No hope,

friends, sleep or
equilibrio for me.

Just Sor, just
studying, so

I study until
dawn's light

surprises me
and my tired brain.

Bigotes and Bellies

A goes with T, C goes with G,
I say when Mr. López Austin

asks me to tell him which DNA
puzzle piece goes with which. I love

biology. I love it when he gives
me something close to a smile

before he goes back to the chalkboard. A regular note, not a plane,

arrives at my desk: *Anamaria goes*
with fat and she has a mustache.

She thinks she's smart, but she's
just ugly. I look around: everyone

is writing. I crumple the note into
a ball and try to focus. Then I feel it:

a blue stare coming from Alexa's eyes.

Toothpick and Olive

At home,
at night, in front

of the mirror, I
stretch my belly

to fit my ribs,
but I can't hold

the extra skin
I've gained since

I turned 13. I used
to be a toothpick

when I was
a kid. Now,

a fat olive
is impaled

by me. But I
feel hungry,

instead of not.
I *should* not, but

in the kitchen
I eat, eat, eat.

Nair Stings

Still up, I apply the thick
cream to my upper lip

to burn my mustache off.
I notice my eyebrows

are like those hairy
worms that burn you. I

think, why not? So I
do, and the sting is

diabolical. Nair
is not made for eye-

brow hair, turns out.
I've destroyed what

Chachita calls mi Arco
del Triunfo, now half-

eyebrows. I've left
the Nair too long:

mi bigote is a pimpled
prairie of burnt skin.

The Next Morning

Chachita holds my face
like an egg, the aloe

stinging more than
soothing the burn.

Chachita blows air
on my face. She smiles,

looking at me like
the Diego Rivera murals

she loves. *Mami, am I
uglier now?* I ask. Her smile

turns into a falling
parachute. *Eres la cosa*

*más bella que he visto
en mi vida,* she replies.

I know I'm not the most
beautiful thing she's seen

in her life. Moms just
say this because they

made and carried
us for nine months!

*But I have a big belly
and a mustache,* I say.

Your belly will melt
away soon, and if not—

Chachita stands up, unzips
part of her pants to show

me her panza. It's not
as flat as I thought.

Do you think I'm ugly?
she asks. *No!* I say.

Then she gets a compact
and twists her short bigotes.

What about now? she asks.
I smile. *Anamaria, you're*

not only beautiful,
you're healthy and

alive. Not every girl
can say that, she says.

She is right: better to be
a bit panzona and hairy,

than pushing daisies.

The Great Bear

The next day at recess, Alexa points at me and says, *You're it, The Great Bear.* I don't get it. No one does. *Are we not bilingual, bola de mensos?* Alexa asks. We, the stupid bunch, just look at each other. *¿La gran osa?* Priscila says in a loud-enough squeak. *Yes ¡La Gran Osa!* Alexa echoes her. No bells ring, bilingual or not. Alexa taps her foot, before she yells, *¡La granosa! The pimply one!* Laughing erupts from every throat, including the prefects' dusty pipes. The door to Principal Martinez's office slams open. *What's going on here?* she shouts, but only half of them are scared into silence. I run to the restroom to cry, the tears itching my pimpled mustache.

"Tía" Thirty

A prefect comes in to the classroom and tells me my aunt is here to take me home. I'm about to say *what aunt?* when I see Thirty.

Me: What do you want, "tía"? I thought you were off helping girls.
Thirty: *A* girl. God, it looks worse than I remember! [she points at my face]

Me: What girl?
Thirty: What will you do about the eyebrows?

Me: *What. Girl.*
Thirty: Don't worry about that. Just don't wait as long as I did to learn how to fill them in [she licks part of her eyebrows off]

Me: How can I *not* worry? *If* you're me, then *I* know the girl.
Thirty: So you believe me now?

Me: No! I said *if.*
Thirty: I think you do. [she singsongs]

Me: ¡Estás descanicada!
Thirty: So now I lost my marbles? Cute.

Me: Tell me!
Thirty: Look, I just wanted you to cut school so you could breathe. So you could talk about what you're going through. And I missed you. I really—

Me: Ahhhhh!
Thirty: What?

I point to a boy's legs dangling from the second story of Sor, his arms and face invisible.

The Gap

A part of Sor's legend is the unfinished
bridge on its second floor that nearly

connects to Principal Martinez's home
so she can, I don't know, run to her

kitchen to concoct her secret Tarahumara
tea? No student has ever used the bridge.

No student is even allowed nearby, so
whoever this boy is, his legs moving

like desperate salted snails, is in deep
trouble, *if* he survives. The gap from

which he dangles is not too high up,
but falling could turn him into a walking

bruise, or depending on what he hits,
mush. *Help, I don't want to die!* the boy

yells. Thirty chuckles as she pats her
pockets. Is there a ladder in her jeans?

My damn iPhone! Thirty curses. *What
phone?!* I ask. *You're useless!* I run

to kick Sor's gate like a mad mule.
Heelp! Heeelp! My lungs spit fire.

Dangling Boy Revealed

Seconds go by before a prefect opens the gate, and it only takes minutes before the firefighter truck's siren deafens the circus attendees: Principal Martinez, some prefects, and every passerby outside of Sor. Thirty stands cross armed. *What? Angry you couldn't eye your phone?* I say, batting my lashes. *I'm just used to having it,* she says. *What is an eye phone?* I ask. Who wouldn't want to know what fits in a pocket and saves dangling boys? *It's IPhone, as in the pronoun, and it's a cellphone. Let me enjoy this,* she says, looking at the boy-saving operation. *Like one of those Nokias rich people have?* She doesn't answer. *Well, you've picked a stupid name for yourPhone!* I say. *Look!* she orders and points at the boy: it's Héctor, who hugs a firefighter for dear life.

"Tía" Out

The crowd on the street is joined by an ambulance and what looks like Héctor's parents.

Me: Did you know he would try to...you know?
Thirty: What?

Me: Try to end it.
Thirty: Héctor was just trying to run away because he didn't do his homework. ¡Qué menso!

Me: How do you know his name?
Thirty: When I was thirteen, I was you. *That's* how I know.

Me: How did you know what he'd do?
Thirty: I heard about it, like everyone else at school. It was funny to actually see him try!

Me: I didn't think so. He could've died.
Thirty: I know, I know! But he was such a spoiled brat.

Me: You're 100% right about that.
Thirty: Who else should we gossip about on your day off?

Me: The girl. Who is she?
Thirty: Leave the girl to me.

Me: Just tell me—is it Pipina? We're no longer friends, but—
Thirty: I *can't* tell you. And you *are* friends. Fight for her and keep working on loving you.

I walk to Principal Martinez to tell her my "aunt" has to leave.

What Loving You Might Be

Science and movies got me closer
to knowing what it means to love

you. Start with what you see
in the mirror and pick one

thing to love. I picked the back
of my head. Since then, I have

thought about adding the color
of my eyes to the list (Mr. Yeyé

says it's pewter and glass). Next
is choosing to live no matter what.

Remember Tristan and the girl
whose heart he broke? She should

have lived. Plus, no boy hurt me,
just four girls: one called me fat

and hairy, one stole my best friend,
one is a poor little rich girl, and one

thinks I'm a cheater. Come to think
of it, it's worse because girls are

better than boys at letting anger
steep for so long, no tea is a match

at numbing tongues. All I really
know is loving *you* is hard, Thirty-

weird, and I always come up
short defining it, but I'm going

to stick it out like a defiant palo
verde growing under the sun.

Voladora de Papantla

It's a record hot spring day in Ciudad Juárez.

    It's also Monday. Principal Martinez
welcomes *First place: Margarita Dospasos*

    Sol. I think about the girl Thirty claims
she will save. *Second place: Héctor Márquez*

    Lara. Dangling boy is not back in school
yet. What if Pipina *is* taken? Is that why Thirty

    told me to fight for her? Will she be...
found? *Third place: Anamaria Aragón Sosa.*

    Could it be Margarita? Priscila? Alexa?
You're third place, wake up! Principal Martinez

    says. I freeze like a watermelon popsicle.
I don't know what to do so I...curtsy. Laughter

    erupts. *Stop it! Go back to class,* Principal
Martinez closes the ceremony. I can't believe

    it: I'm honor roll royalty. I'm a Papantla
flier. The air tickles my brave, flying feet!

Tamarindo Feelings

Silence rules Sor's 7th grade when Héctor
        comes back to school. *What?*
he confronts all of us. Some laughter gets
        out. *I didn't do homework. It was*
an escape attempt. The only one in Sor's
        history! Better to run than face you-
know-who, he says. Cheers and clapping.
        Thirty knew this. How? *Is this*
a zoo? Principal Martinez's thick figure
        appears by our classroom door.
No clapping: new rule, she barks. Alexa
        raises her hand and says, *Héctor*
is our hero. He survived! How can we honor
        him? Principal Martinez stares her
down and says, *You shake your palm like*
        you do a tambourine! Nail polish is
not allowed. I told your parents once. Come
        with me. I grin, shameless. Alexa
sees me. A feeling like sucking on tamarindo
        candy rises to my throat. Sweet:
Alexa *has* broken the rules for too long.
        Sour: she's mean, but maybe she
is sad like me. Maybe she's in danger as in
        the girl Thirty says she's saving.

Héctor, You Stupid Boy

Mr. López Austin writes "chemical elements quiz" on the board. It's been weeks since we studied that, so the tension could be cut like lard. *Ms. Dospasos Sol, tell us the formula for carbon dioxide, plus chemical elements and atomic weights,* he says from the chalkboard. *C for Carbon, O—O for Oxygen,* Margarita starts, but can't finish her litany of middle school chemistry. *Fail,* I almost hear the class say. I want her to beat them, but Margarita's skin turns eggshell. *I guess first place is up for grabs now!* Héctor says, looking at Margarita, expecting a smile. Is there a limit to how stupid some boys can be? Mr. López Austin's *Stop!* does nothing to lower the arms that shake their palms to silent-clap. Margarita's inner daisy loses petals.

Soda and Salsa SOS

At El Colorín, I feel a need to call Pipina, but her landline says busy or gone after five tries. *Allow more than one minute between calls,* Chachita says, pinching my cheek before going back to work. My mouth turns into an old lemon. I go to the soda fountain to wash away the acid with a Sprite-Fanta-Manzanita mix. My sickly-sweet tongue goes numb, so I eat salsa and chips. My stomach gurgles *stop.* I had five tacos on the sly before this. I run to the restroom where I turn on the faucet and drink water like dogs do, splashing my Sor uniform. My El Colorín desk is set up, and homework waits for me. But all I can think about is Pipina and Margarita.

Pencil Knife

Moonlight filtering
through my curtains

tells me it's late. My
bloated belly

hurts, and I
can't sleep. I

find my back-
pack in the darkness

and do homework
until I swear

the pencil
in my hand turns

into a knife.
The sugar and spice

from before burns
my throat. I run

to the bathroom
and throw up.

Hateful Sunday

Sunday is not church day for us because Sundays in El Colorín are busy. Sundays, I sink my teeth into my homework like some people eat the holy wafer: slowly. Sometimes I go to Mr. Yeyé's afterwards to help him bake for Monday's early rush. Now I go to escape the noise, the food, the soda fountain and salsa bar. I knock like you do on a priest's confession box. The sun is merciless and Mr. Yeyé's not opening. I hate sweating like a pig. I hate my shadow. She's thinner and fresher than me. The door opens. Inside, I hate the syrupy, hot air. I sit down, mute. He offers me a plate with fresh marranitos. *Take it away, I'm fat!* I say and stand up. I want to run, but I can't go anywhere alone. *I hate this city! I hate Thirty! I hate myself!* I confess, beating my chest.

Thirty is a Butterfly

Mr. Yeyé tells me that cleaning windows relaxes him. I'm not looking to poke holes in his logic right now, so I ask for Windex and newspaper. Mr. Yeyé says to take *all* the time in the world. I obey: erase and draw streak marks. Erase and draw—

Thirty: ¡Hola, Sr. Yeyé! [he waves quickly, goes back to kneading dough]
Me: [I continue erasing and drawing]

Thirty: Hey you.
Me:

Thirty: Cat got your tongue? [she chuckles]
Me: [erasing and drawing]

Thirty: Hey! Stop that for a second!
Me:

Thirty: What's wrong? Talk to me. Please.
Me: [I put the Windex down and crumple the wet newspaper in my fist]

Thirty: I'm here to help.
Me: I don't like cats.

Thirty: OK. So—
Me: I don't have friends. I'm seeing things.

Thirty: What did you see?
Me: A knife, but it was my pencil.

Thirty: Did you talk to Chachita and Papiringo?
Me: No, I can't!

Thirty: You can. You just have to try. Now, let's look for the positive side of this.
Me: That's corny *and* stupid!

Thirty: Calm down. Look, that didn't happen to me until I was in my twenties. Maybe—
Me: *Maybe* I've been right all along. You're you. I'm me.

Thirty: Or maybe my being here is changing things. Like the butterfly effect.
Me: What is that?

Thirty: One little event, like the flapping of a butterfly's wings, can cause a hurricane somewhere.
Me: Who is who in this set up?

Thirty: I came here from the future, so maybe I'm the butterfly?
Me: Oh, so *I'm* the hurricane?

Thirty: Who cares! Maybe this is good, you know?
Me: How? *Everything* is falling apart.

Thirty: I'm here now and it'll get better. You have to learn to see the silver lining.
Me: Maybe I should "see" myself down Sor's unfinished bridge.

Thirty: What?
Me: Nothing. I'm tired of being me. That's all.

Thirty: You are wonderful, Anamaria. Believe it.
Me: Can I clean some windows please? [half-heartedly, I throw the wet ball of newspaper at her]

Heart/Off

Pipina laughs with Priscila, showing
her chewed lunch to the world. I close

my eyes and cling to the sound. Fudd
sliced ham is my favorite, but now

it tastes like spiced plastic between two
slices of bread. The grape juice I drink

to wash it away with is sour. A shadow
blocks the sun. *You're friends with her,*

right? Héctor says, putting his hands
inside his pockets and looking around

to make sure no one sees him talking
to the pimply girl, even though most

of the pimples have faded. *If you mean*
Margarita, no. Not anymore. Go away

now, I say, staring at my lunch. *Anamaria,*
please, I really like her and she won't talk

to me after what I said in class, Héctor says.
Alexa taps his shoulder, giving me rabid

possum eyes. *Héctor, you shouldn't go*
near her. She's contagious, she says.

I was just telling her to go see the doctor,
and get a new face or something, Héctor

replies without true meanness in his eyes.
I say, *Like in Face/Off? I'd go for Travolta's*

face. You? Alexa scoffs. Héctor
chuckles. *Fat and funny. Great mix,*

she says before pulling him by his arm.
I turn to see Pipina's eyes on me. I want

to smile, but my heart has forgotten how.

Letter for Pipina

You're the heart to my tin man. You're the courage to my lion. You're the brain to my scarecrow. This makes you Dorothy. We're not in Kansas. We're in Ciudad Juárez, trapped in Sor. Click, click, your red shoes go. I'm the Wicked Witch of the West. My mean girl ways flying monkeys. My green face envy. Priscila is your Toto now. Does she go woof-woof? Can her voice go that high? Has she made any other weird-shaped cakes? Back to Oz. The Wizard would be Thirty. She's a secret of sorts. She says she's from the future. She says she's me. But she's a poet who limps, so it can't be me. Tangent alert! Point is I'm sorry for everything. For not saying sorry sooner. The Yellow Brick Road has never been thornier, if you catch my drift. I wish a click click of your shoes could bring us together. Forever. I love you. Anamaria Aragón Sosa [future doctor signature]

Letter for Pipina 2

You're the heart to my ███████████████████████████████████
███
███ *Wicked*
Witch of the West. ███
███
███
███
███ *I'm*
sorry for everything. For not saying sorry sooner. The Yellow Brick Road has
never been thornier, if you catch my drift. █████████████████████
████████████████████████ *I love you. Anamaria Aragón Sosa* [*future*
doctor signature]

Letter for Pipina 3

 I'm sorry for everything. love you. Anamaria

Pipina's Cup of Tea

Papiringo says that Chachita
used to look like Ali MacGraw,

who starred in *Love Story,*
a movie that always ends in

Kleenex, more Kleenex, please!
from my crying papis. Always

distracted by their teary plight, I
never thought too much about

the lovers' soundbite, *Love means
never having to say you're sorry,*

until now: If Pipina knew how much
she means to me, she would know

that I love her, that I'm sorry, that I
need her. Forget about what I said

that time! The Oz telegram-like
letter shouldn't be needed at all.

But I forget *again* that Pipina's
cup of tea is candy, drawing and

jokes. No sour leaves. No honor.

Honor Roll Princess

This Monday at Sor is also the first day of the month
        so I mumble *Bandera de México* while
placing my palm perpendicular to my chest and
        hiding my yawns. *Chirp. Chirrrrp.* My ears
spike up. Why did I never hear the crickets' song
        before? I guess my ears are working overtime
while I'm in zombie mode. I wonder if I could catch
        one to have a pet. A friend. Crickets can't be
too messy. *First place: Margarita Dospasos Sol.*
        Do crickets eat leaves? I feel eyes on me.
Is second place not enough to earn a response
        from you, Ms. Aragón Sosa? the principal
asks. I just nod, and remember to not curtsy. *Third*
        place: Priscila Palacios Allende. Palms go
up in the air and turn. The no-clapping rule has held.
        Chirp, chirp, the crickets congratulate me.

I Want to Fly

Like Dios, Mr. López Austin
forgives my sins now that I'm

one place away from first
by saying *felicidades* from

his desk. I walk to my seat on
a cloud that doesn't let me see

Alexa pushing her backpack
to trip me. My hands break

the fall. My knees and my shins
too. The collective gasp and stifled

laughter activate a tear hose
and siren mode. I hear my own

wah-wah-cartoon-like sobs as if
a winged doppelganger watched

perched on the window sill.
Forget the dumb palo verdes.

I *don't* want to "stick it out"!
Two arms touch my back,

and glue the body-mind split.
It's Pipina and Priscila trying

to stop my social suicide.
Let go of me. ¡No me toquen!

I say, their kindness leprosy.
I run to the door like a headless

gallina and go outside looking for
anyone who loves me in the halls

of Sor. I hear the prefects' *Stop!*
as I climb the second floor,

but my feet fly. I stop when I
see yellow tape that says "caution"

to block the famous gap between
the school and the principal's house.

It's so thin, I rip it with my hands.
No escape attempt for me. I want

to fly to a purple, bruised end.
One, two, three. One, two, three,

I count. *Where do you think you
are going?* I hear the principal's

tapping of her heavy brown heels,
and somehow, my burning feet

lose the wings and will to jump.

Help?

I think your daughter needs some...help.
I can hear the principal's voice
even though I'm sitting outside her office,
        where I notice a plastic ficus being
the closest thing to life. *This behavior is not*
        tolerated here. Anamaria is one of our
brightest, but tantrums like these are wrong.
        Protests coming from Chachita are
nipped in the bud like weeds. The principal
        continues, *Either she calms down or*
she's out. Sor can't deal with this...these...
        things. Take her with you. Talk some
sense into her. A prefect will have her home-
        work packet. Good day. Chachita's
and Papiringo's scraping chairs are as
        defeated as them. I leave nail marks
on the ficus' fake leaves. What does
        help look like? Who can help me? Thirty?

The Vent Spills

Cursing and clearing wet throats.

Papiringo	Chachita
¿Qué hacemos?	
	I don't know. Talk to her?
Will that be enough?	
	And how? Do we just say— *were you trying to—to…*
Hurt yourself?	
	But why would she? She told *me she was happy.*
I don't know, but *she's always been—*	
	What?
You know, too—too…	
	Too hard on herself. Too *focused on grades. I thought* *that we were blessed to have a* *child who knows school is* *important, but she has* *become…obsessed.*
What if she leaves Sor?	
	She won't like it.
¡No importa! We have *to help her.*	
	We do.
We'll talk to her *in the morning.*	
	We will do it with café, so it *feels "grown up."*
Eso le va encantar.	
	She will love it, and *she will be fine.*
She will be great.	
	She will be happy.

A kiss or hug ends their talk.
I hope they sleep. My eyes become
stuck on the popcorn white ceiling.

Magic Tricks

All night I think in circles: mis papis, Sor, mis papis, Sor. I think until my hair hurts: should I lock my room, should I run away, should I try to jump again, for good? Should I try to talk to Thirty when she takes a break from rescuing this girl? The early sun of summer sparks quicker fixes in my brain. *Preparation H.* Chachita uses it to make puffy eyes depuff. *Pigtails.* Happy girls start with happy hair. *Smile.* Fake it till you make it, Americans say. *Blush.* My cheeks match the gray of my eyes. I pinch my cheeks hard because Chachita's Maybelline is gone. *High pitch and giggles.* Buenos días, I feel so much better! *Hope.* A trick you can perform for others. *Abracadabra.* Mis papis don't take me out of Sor and I still get some coffee.

Jumping Girl Strikes

Pigtails are not allowed, Alexa yells,
circling me like a vulture at recess.

It's been a week since she tripped me,
but she's not satisfied. Prefects have

eyed my hair style, and they eye us
now, but they don't say anything.

I'm "jumping girl" now. I heard their
pity through a loud, murmured song

in the halls. I wonder why Héctor
didn't have to deal with this, even

if his was an escape attempt. *Hey,
I'm talking to you, Great Bear!*

Alexa yells, trying to elicit thunder
storms, or at least isolated showers.

Prefects lock their knees, stuck in place.
I don't want Chachita and Papiringo

to visit the principal again so I ask
her to come closer to whisper, *You*

are pretty, but so sad. I'm sorry.
Her face becomes a Picasso sketch.

Raw Dough

I ask Mr. Yeyé (who's all elbow grease)
        about Thirty. He says she hasn't
dropped by in a while, but last time he
        saw her she looked like a gancho:
a human hanger for her flesh and clothes.
        He says that when his niece went
missing, his sister looked like Thirty: skinny,
        ragged. I don't know what to say.
Like a robot, I see him putting a piece of
        raw dough he's been rolling in his
mouth. He spits it out, and says *¡Ay Dios!*
        I still don't know what to say, and
I know God will probably not answer him,
        so I eat a piece myself. *Mm, these
will sell!* I say. Mr. Yeyé smiles crooked.
        Tears like dew sprout from his eyes.

Busy Thirty

Thirty limps in looking exactly as Mr. Yeyé described. She asks Mr. Yeyé for two marranitos and café de olla, no milk.

Me: Looking enchanting.
Thirty: You know [half-chewed pig says hi], sarcasm is the weapon of the weak.

Me: I—
Thirty: I know I look bad. Just say that instead.

Me: I'm sorry.
Thirty: That's a first.

Me: Where have you been?
Thirty: I've been trying to "butterfly" things.

Me: If you say so.
Thirty: How's your hurricaning going?

Me: Swell!
Thirty: Swell? Enchanting? Oh, and I'm loving the pigtails.

Me: You know what they say about sarcasm...
Thirty: [she chuckles] Fair enough. Would you read this? It's probably very bad.

Me: Why me?
Thirty: Because I care what you think. By the way, the Preparation H will stop working.

Me: How did you know about—

Thirty: Busy. Bye! [she taps my head like a dog on her way out]

Thirty's Poem

The night eats the sky, and even roaches
hide when I try to fight the wind,
dust and hunger that split the balance
of my stick-like right leg. But I must
do something for her. I stand watch like
a stupid owl over her neighborhood,
waiting for my eyes and neck
to catch the bad: steps
that shouldn't echo at night, cars
whose engines shouldn't break
the orchestra of the shivering
leaves. I feel the earth join the quiet
ripple reaching my chest. My cartilage-
starved meniscus cracks some more. But I
must do something to save her. The cold
asphalt meets my buttocks and I know
sleep has come to collect.
The night eats me whole.

— Thirty, Ciudad Juárez, "1999"

Strikethrough

I eat cucumbers with salt and lime in El Colorín, then I sharpen my pencil.

The night eats the sky, ~~and even roaches~~
~~hide when I try to fight the wind,~~
~~dust, and hunger~~ [1] that split the balance
of my stick-like right knee. But I must
do something for ~~her~~. [2] I stand watch like
~~a stupid owl~~ [3] over her neighborhood,
waiting for my eyes and neck
to catch the ~~bad~~ [4]: steps
that shouldn't echo at night, cars
whose engines shouldn't break
the orchestra of the shivering
leaves. I feel the earth joining the quiet
ripple reaching my chest. ~~My cartilage-~~
~~starved meniscus cracks some more.~~[5] But I
must do something to save ~~her~~ [2(again)] The
cold asphalt meets my buttocks and I know
sleep has come to collect.
The night eats me whole.

¹ Cockroaches are afraid of nothing:
they have wings, they love garbage,
they will survive nuclear war.

² No clues for "her": faceless pronouns
are a waste of time. A name is better.
A face is best.

³ Owls' necks are magic swivels.
Owls are wise. Killing this symbol
is not kind or precise!

⁴ "Bad" is as bland and confusing as "her."
Bad who?

⁵ Calling all medical encyclopedias to help!
Overkill. We get it: you a have a limp!

—Anamaria, Ciudad Juárez, definitely 1999

Priscila is God

A set of teenage, well-oiled knees kneel
beside me. *You think I'm sad?* Alexa

hisses, *Look at yourself! You're—*
Alexa, stop! Priscila commands,

her frizzy hair hot with the coil
of girlhood. *Your mom can't stand*

listening to you. Maybe that's why
you talk, talk, talk! Alexa's body

gives way to that of a creature too
little and frail to fight back. She runs

to hide in the restroom. I think about
the saying: look at people with awe,

like jackrabbits look at God. This is
how I look at Priscila now: mighty

and good, towering over me. *De nada,*
she says, not waiting for the "thanks"

I should've said because I'm still too
small and furry as I watch this girl-

turned-God join Pipina on their patch
of cement. Alexa's sobs reach every ear.

A Paper Plane Carries a Pinky Promise

A note lands like a drunk plane on my desk:
        Maybe you were right about Héctor.
I turn to find Margarita's half-smile meet
        my blank face. *Maybe,* I write back.
The note passes hands to reach her. Margarita's
        wrist moves furiously. I read the results.
I'm sorry I yelled. I felt embarrassed and mad.
        I don't let anyone get to me. But you
are my friend, and it hurt. Please come over
        this weekend. Cecy and Brenda won't
stop asking about you. They're driving me as
        loca as the life your idol sings about.
p.s. Ricky Martin loves Anamaria. I read her
        note so many times, I feel dizzy when
the bell to leave rings. *So? Friends again?*
        For good? Margarita says, holding her
pinky finger like we did when we were kids.
        My pinky and heart squeeze back.

The Vent Leaks

A loud round between mis papis.

               Papiringo   Chachita

I don't want her to
go there again.

                    But she needs friends.

That's where the last
girl was taken!

                    Girls are being taken all over
                    the place!

Maybe, but—

                    Yeyé's niece didn't live there!

But she's still dead.

A pin drops.

¡Abre los ojos! You know
which girls are taken
the most.

                    My eyes are open. Poor girls
                    are taken the most, but
                    Anamaria can't stop
                    living her life!

If she went missing,
do you think anyone else
but us would care? These
lost girls are just blood
and ink posters no one
does anything about!

                    Shh! You'll wake her up!

Can't the friend
come here?

Our neighborhood is not
much safer.

Says who?

You! Everyone! We're
poor too!

Yes, but—

Ciudad Juárez is our home even
if it's far from perfect and we
have a daughter who needs friends!

A Perfect Heart

Papiringo drives me to Margarita's house
in a silence broken only by the brakes

of his truck. *We never leave her house
to have fun,* I say to cut him a slice

of the peace pie he needs. I wave to him
from Margarita's door to wave away

a fear I can't understand because I'm not
a mom or a dad. Cecy and Brenda jump,

as if with springs, when they see me come
in. *You must swim with us this time!* Brenda

says with the voice of a woman, not a five-
year-old girl. *My sister is outside,* Cecy

says. To the right, the backyard door
opens to a medium-sized above-ground

pool squished into a space fit for a picnic
table. To the left, some cages. *It's rabbits!*

You want to see them? Cecy leads me to
our meet-and-greet with the big-toothed,

massive creatures. *Hey, remember, she's
my friend too,* Margarita yells as she

submerges her legs in the water,
singing the score for *Jaws.*

Brenda squeals with more Milky Way
Joy. In this slice of world, these girls

and I are nothing but rich. May we be
safe, may we grow up, I pray, even

though I still don't know how. A feeling,
strong like vinegar, makes my eyes water.

I know they smell, Cecy says. *I want
gray eyes like yours when I'm older.*

You two, play shark with us! Margarita
interrupts us. A squirming Bugs leaves

my arms before I can tell Cecy beauty
lives in her big brown eyes. The weak

steel of my irises is just a pretty lack
of pigment that I would trade her in

a flash for her perfect heart which
flutters when she joins her sisters,

pruned by chlorine, in the moving water.

Héctor, You Stupid Boy 2

We eat a lot of Pollo Loco
for dinner again. I don't mind:

I like roasted chicken, especially
if salsa verde smothers it. Cecy

and Brenda's energy bursts
into a nap so quick, so full

of peace, Margarita and I follow
along. For the first time in months,

I crave for a mattress to hug me
into rest, not a Morse-code night

of homework and choppy sleep. We lay
flat on our backs, suspended between

the floor and our dreams as if
by threads woven by God. *Ring!*

Margarita jumps to her feet, whispers
sorry, before leaving. Her muffled

voice sounds jumpy. I tiptoe into the hall,
hidden, but close enough to hear "Héctor."

Stupid boy: are you begging for perdón?

A New Honor Roll Queen

It's another Monday. Spring is gone, and summer
          says he's king. Principal Martinez's knee-
length skirt stands immobile, ready to announce us
          like racing dogs. I'm so tired, I focus on
the crickets' seesaw-cello song to not fall asleep
          while standing up. *First place*—I've seen
cricket farms in pet stores in Rio Grande Mall—
          Anamaria Aragón Sosa. They were cool.
They're calling you, Pipina whispers. The gasps
          mute the crickets. *Second place: Margarita*
*Dospasos Sol. Third place: Priscila...*I'm happy
          for me, for all of us, but will I lose Margarita
over this? The crickets' chirping takes over again.
          It scratches my ears like nails on glass.

I Don't Care

about first

place. I care
about

a place
in your home,

with you,
your sisters,

your rabbits,
your pool.

I write a poem
in my head

before I see
Margarita

in the classroom.
The words are

ready to jump
off my tongue

but she stops
them with

a high five.

Chocolate Cake and Apologies

To celebrate first place, Chachita bakes a Betty Crocker chocolate cake, which is rare. She hates measuring cups and baking. Chachita says it's movie time. Channel 32 is our favorite. Her thin arms envelop me, and I smell the salt and sugar on her skin. *I wonder what's playing,* she says. I'm not sure I care. The only thing that's missing is Papiringo, but one of them has to be in El Colorín. *¡El Mago de Oz!* Chachita shouts. I smile and hug her tight, tight. This is a bit too on the nose. Pipina's Oz letter is still in my Composition. That movie, *Love Story,* was wrong. I have to apologize *because* I love Pipina. Will she forgive me? There's only one way to know.

The End of My World?

I find Pipina before the first Sor bell
rings. We were always early birds.

We feared the face-to-face punctuality
talk with Principal Martinez. I give her

the first letter: hungry, afraid. I wanted
to make it pretty, draw something, but

I didn't want to offend Pipina's artistic
sensibilities. Her eyes move to read

each line. I feel my hands sweating.
If she doesn't forgive me, this could be

the end of the world. *My* world. If—
She gives me a Mexican hug: full

and never-ending. Tears draw paths
of relief on my cheeks. *I'm sorry,*

I'm sorry, I'm sorry, I whisper.
Do you want to come watch Sixth

Sense this Friday at Multicinemas
with me and Priscila? Pipina says.

Yes, please! I say, still hugging her,
and catching a glimpse of Margarita.

The Pipina + Margarita Project

I eat my lunch with Margarita
who is quieter than usual. I see

her from the corner of my eye.
To be a girl and have friends

that are girls is a rigged mamaleche
game where lines are redrawn every

minute. I look to her bologna, cheese
and mustard sandwich for a metaphor

to save us: *Mustard can accompany*
so many foods, like hot dogs, burgers.

She holds a hand to my face. *Stop. If*
you don't need me now that you and she

are friends again, I—I understand. This
mustard can do well by herself, Margarita

says. *But you're my friend too. And you*
used to be friends with her. ¿Qué pasó?

I ask. *You know what happened,* she says
and scoffs. I press on, *You know Pipina*

doesn't care about money! Sometimes
she just talks without thinking. But we

could help her understand our
worlds are different than hers, I

plead. Margarita says nothing.
Admit it: you and I need her

lightness to dilute our...whatever
it is, so let's go to the movies with

her and Priscila! I say. *¡Ándale!*
C'mon! I poke her ribs. Her round

cheeks form a heart with her chin:
No promises. But I'll ask my parents.

Sixth Sense

At the movies, Pipina, Priscila and I eat our nails instead of popcorn. I can't see Chachita, our "invisible" nanny, but I'm sure she's doing the same. I draw blood from my finger when "Cole" of *Sixth Sense* says he sees dead people. Before that, he was just a character who only had bullies, no friends, and who ate celery and milk for dinner with his chatty mom. I'm breathing easy, then a vomiting dead girl jumps onto the screen. I look to my right to see Pipina and Priscila covering their eyes with their hands. I look to my left where Margarita would've sat. I wish she were here. We waited for her in the lobby until Chachita said to go on our own while she stayed behind. I bet she would have said, *It's not that scary, relax!*

Have You Seen My Daughter?

Sixth Sense is
ending. Cole itches

to spill an awful
truth— *Have you*

seen my daughter?
a voice, wet

and desperate,
fills the theater.

A collective shush.
Have. You. Seen.

My. Daughter?! I
turn to see two small

bodies hanging on
to a larger one.

My throat dries. Cecy
finds me and says,

She ran to take the bus,
angry, when mamá said

we didn't have money
for the movies. Is she here?

Bullet Point Girl

Missing posters hang on windows and street lights. Squashed bugs have more color than her sad Sor yearbook picture. The bullet points don't help me recognize her, so how would anyone else in this city full of missing girls?

- *Height: 1.60m.*
- *Eyes and hair: brown and black.*
- *Skin: morena.*
- *Distinguishing features: high cheeks with acne spots.*
- *Last seen: in her house.*

What could I do to make the image of her speak? Nothing. I spend a week of recess scratching my knuckles raw, un-moved by anything, anyone. I spend days and nights writing. Doing more nothing.

Daisy, Margarita

where you are,
I want to be.
Is it crazy
to want,
to dream,
that you ran
away with milky
Héctor? To wish
you two lived in
a house that has
oak desks for
you to study on
and ten Olympic
pools to play
shark in? We
hurt for you
to be here. Cecy
and Brenda wait
for you to open
the door, and play
until they can
play no more.
First place is
yours. You are
the only honor
roll queen.

Mother Beast

Ciudad Juárez, I love you, but I didn't feel
the blood on your face until now. Can you

see your lost and killed? Can you see
Margarita? Does the pupil of your heart

bleed for them or are you blind? Juan Gabriel
says that you're number one. At what?

Your potholes? Crooked streets? Unmarked
sewers? Is that where all the girls are?

Are they feeding on dirty water, dust
and rats? Ciudad Juárez, you're my other

madre and I ask you now: do you grieve
with us like a mother? Couldn't you turn

on your flickering street lights to have
your old eyes on them? Juan Gabriel's

voice is gone. The eagle and serpent
have flown the cactus, the nest. You,

madre. It hurts to love you, Ciudad Juárez:
you're a red cruel beautiful mother beast.

Punchline

Chachita and Papiringo send me to Mr. Yeyé after school, who looks at
me in nervous ten-second spurts. I understand why: I bring my missing
friend to join his dead niece. His usual dough scent smells sour. He
doesn't wave when Thirty comes in.

Thirty: Anamaria—
Me: Is this the punchline?

Thirty: What?
Me: To you being here.

Thirty: I tried to save her. I stood watch every day. I—
Me: Stop. Disappear. Go back to where, "when" you belong.

Thirty: I *fought* to save her! I watched her house at night. That's what
the poem is about.
Me: So what happened? "Stupid owl" eyes got too tired?

Thirty: [tears fill the rim of her eyes]
Me: Or were you too busy writing poems?

Thirty: Of course not—
Me: How could you lose her?

Thirty: I'm so sorry, I— Everything changed! The butterfly effect—
Me: This is *your* fault, not an insect's!

Thirty: [wailing comes out of her]
Mr. Yeyé: What's happening here, Anamaria? [he runs over, napkins
flapping from his hands]

Punchbag

Anamaria, please, eat with us,
Pipina pleads, pulling my sleeve.

Recess is my time to seethe,
to make my eyes crunch

dry from staring at Margarita's
Missing Poster. *Ey, ¿cómo estás?*

Héctor asks, his voice a blip. I turn
to see all of 7th grade staring at me

from their stupid corners. I turn
to see his milky face. *Did you know*

she was taken because of her cinder
block house? Because she had a small

pool, not an Olympic one, like you? I
accuse him. Héctor's thinking, but I'm

quicker than him. *Is that why she's gone,*
and not her? I say, pointing to Alexa,

who must be loving the scene even
though she looks like ash. She walks

over. *Tsk, tsk, Great Bear. First places*
are supposed to be smart. Your friend

was dirt poor, yes, but what else?
Look at yourself. Think! Alexa says,

her voice dry and hot. She waits for
me to do as she says, but I don't know

what she means. She grabs my arm, and
puts it next to hers. *Look at us! We are*

light-skinned. White. She was dark. Most
dead girls are. Look at the missing posters:

it's like seeing double. Triple! Wake up!
Alexa says, letting go of my arm. I try

the old 1-to-10 count as I feel my hands
curling into balls. *I saw her mooning over*

Héctor. That was never happening.
Be thankful someone killed that dream

for her! Alexa says. I feel numbers
nine and ten escaping the grooves

of my boiling brain before my
fist finds her white, white face.

Poor Girls

Who's in charge of El Colorín? I ask Chachita and Papiringo after we don't turn on Adolfo López Mateos street. Neither of them replies. They picked me up from Sor after Principal Martinez called them. We get home. *Wait!* Chachita says to stop the march to my room, *I know you're going through something—but you've been suspended, and that poor girl was rushed to the dentist.* Papiringo's canary is mute. *Maybe—*but *that 'poor girl' said Margarita was taken because she was poor and morena, and I'm only safe because of the color of my skin,* I spit out. The white in Chachita's eyes is inflamed with thick red threads.

Breaking Girls

Home is like a glass
castle: one sudden

sound and it will
break. I wait to hear

through the vent
that mis papis

are tired of me even if
they love me. But, how

could they love
me, a breaker

of girls' teeth?
Ciudad Juárez is

already so
broken by

bodies
of girls

and women in
the middle

of the desert. What
have I become?

Zero

I am a zero. Nada.

I am a zero daughter and friend.

(proof: missing Margarita. proof: hurting

Pipina). I am   the zeros in

my 100s.   A grade.

A number.   Nothing else.

Not even   H0n0r. She

is nothing   too: just a lie

a dream   a whisper of

who is best.   Who is top

(lonely) dog.   I am a zero:

fat but empty   of a young

good heart. I have a charcoal instead

inside. The zeroes in me cry

Ooooo, Ooooo, Oooo.

Margalexa

I dream of Margarita.
She jumps from Sor's

second floor. A pool
of crickets with knives

for legs breaks her
fall. I jump after her,

my thrashing arms
covered with cuts.

She emerges, eye-
less, covered in thick

white paint, her
hair tangled with

blonde broom
bristles. *I'm Alexa.*

Be my friend? she
says with a tooth-

less grin. I wake
up, shivering.

I run to find
my Composition.

Poem to Chachita and Papiringo

Mami y papi.
I am sorry I drew
blood from a girl.
Even if the girl
spoke venom. Even
if the girl drew blood
from me when she
tripped me. Even—
This is me: no sleep,
just bad dreams, doing
homework at night.
Eating everything
in sight. I heard you
through the vent: I fit
a category of lost
girl: "poor." I
don't fit the morena
one. But: a girl is
a girl is a girl.
This means—I am
not sure what it means,
but I am sorry. I will
be a better me for you.

Poem to Chachita

Mami █████
I am sorry I █████
███████████████
███████████
spoke venom. Even
if the girl drew blood
████████████████
████████████
This is me: █████
  just █████
████████████████
homework █ *night.*
Eating █████████
████████████████
████████████████
███████████████
██ [and] "poor" [girl]
████████████████
██ *But: a girl is*
a girl is a girl.
This means— █████
████████████████
███████████ *I will*
be a better me for you.

Poem to Papiringo

██████ *Papi,*
I am sorry I ██████
████████████
████████████
█████████████
██████████████
████████████
████████████

This is me: no sleep,
just ████████
████████████
█████████ *night.*
████████████
██████ *I heard you*
through the vent: I ██
████████████
[=] *"poor"* [girl] ██
█████████████
███ *But:*
████████████
████████████
███████████████
█████████████ *I will*
be a better me for you.

Poem to Me

[Anamaria] ██████████

██████████

██████████

██████████

██████████

███████████

██████████

███████████

██████████

██████████████

██████████

██████████

██████████

████████████ [you] fit
a category [:] ██████ [sad]
girl ██████

███████████████

██ But: a girl is
a girl is a girl.
This means — ████ [girls
are the same. Or so I
I thought. For now, I
██████████ I will
just be] ██████ me.

Girl

What is a girl? Her color, her skin, her face, her eyes, her cheeks, her brain, her belly, her mami, her papi, her money, her anger, her joy, her life, her death? I think not. Girls are not word banks, bullet points, summaries or headlines. Girls are stories. I think. But will all stories be told? Will all stories be read? Will all stories have an end? I don't know. Alexa said as much when Margarita's story was spit in three words: poor, dark, missing. This has me going in mad-sad circles because I don't or can't understand. Is it just luck if we can't choose to be born rich and white? Does that turn the unlucky into bruised apples who face a dead-end life in the trash? This has me spinning in ugly unfair circles, with no way out. Not even in biology where a girl is just a mute icon: an O above a hanging cross. Our stories a pen scratch. That's why I use a heart: to feel my pulse, an answer: a girl is a human.

It

The crickets' uneven song
is loud in Sor's yard. What

could this meeting be about
if expelled has to be *it* for me

after punching Alexa? Words
drip from Principal Martinez's

lips like bitter tree sap until she
says, *If you want to stay in Sor*

then you have to sing. I pinch
myself to see if this is a death

dream. It's not. Why does she
think I can do this? I mean, I

sang in the sad, small Sor choir
in elementary school and soloed

once or twice before Sor deemed
singing useless. But that was years

ago! Why now? *Sor has to compete*
in every contest, she says, reading

my mind. *Do you need water? My*
fake ficus looks more alive than you!

It Details

Song: "Buenos días, señor sol." The whole
        city knows about Sor's kill joy,
ambitious ways. Does Principal Martinez
        think a feel-good song will give me
an edge? Songwriter: Juan Gabriel. Forgive
        me, Juanga. I will flay your words
with my pipes. Contest: Middle School
        Regional Singing Olympics. When:
In a week. Catch 1: I still don't sing. Fairy
        dust is in short supply. Catch 2:
No singing teacher. Not that we have one.
        I'm to practice alone. Does shower-
singing like most people who are not Christina
        Aguilera count? Catch 3 (in case I
forgot): sing "proud" for Sor, plus keep 1st
        place on the honor roll or it's bye
sayonara adiós Anamaria baby be gone.

Wailing Girl

I'm back at Sor. My backpack
feels alien against my spine.

I run into Mr. López Austin in
the yard. He half-smiles then

Houdinis his way out of sight.
From the restroom, wailing

comes. I go inside. She tries
the feet-on-toilet trick to hide.

¿Estás bien? I ask, walking
into the stall next to hers. *Hey,*

talk to me. I won't tell anyone,
I say. La Llorona's cries sound

like whispers next to this girl's.
No-one-no-one-understands-me-

and-no-one-loves-me, she says,
Not-even-my-mom-I'm-so-hungry-

I-am-so-tired-I-want-to-I-want-
to-die. ¿Me en-tien-des? I say yes

because, for better or worse,
I really, truly do understand.

Wailing Girl Revealed

Who are you? the girl asks. *Anamaria, you?* The girl comes out. She kicks my door open. Alexa's face is pockmarked by crying welts. *As if my tooth wasn't enough! Look, it's fake now!* she says, pointing to her front tooth. It looks like a Chiclet. *Hit me, I deserve it,* I say, offering my face to her. Her knuckles rise. I close my eyes and wait. And wait. I peek and see her hair is wilting blonde. Her eyes, a blue that hurts. *Why are you hungry?* I ask. *You heard my mom. I'm fat. So I don't eat much. I'm ugly. So I wear lip gloss and paint my nails. But. I'm more than this, I—*she says, looking at the floor. *You're not ugly. You're not even pretty. You're beautiful,* I say. Her smile is weak. *I'm sorry. For everything. But. No one loves me. I just want it to stop,* she says as she leaves.

Alarm Clock

I wake up to Chachita's voice and Juan Gabriel's words.

Todas las mañanas que	Every morning Mr. Sun
entra por mi ventana	enters my window
el señor sol, doy gracias a	I thank God for
Dios por otro día más.	another day.
Hoy como otros días,	Today, like all days,
yo seguiré tratando	I will keep trying
ser mejor y sonriendo	my best and smiling I
haré las cosas con amor.	will do things with love.
¡Buenos días alegría,	Good morning, joy!
buenos días al amor!	Good morning, love!
¡Buenos días a la vida,	Good morning, life!
buenos días señor sol!	Good morning, Mr. Sun!

Some people sing to pray, Chachita says, kissing my head.
Sing for Margarita.

Dancing Margarita

I tap the microphone. *Hola, ¿cómo están todos?* I ask like a third-rate Mexican Oprah. My shirt sticks to my armpits. Several throats clear. *Esto es 'Buenos días señor sol' por Juan Gabriel,* I say, lifting my fist with Juarense pride. Nothing. I start to sing and feel coals burning my cheeks. My voice shakes. When the line *Doy gracias a Dios por otro día más* comes, I couldn't be less grateful to God. I feel tar running down my back. I raise my free hand and move it from side to side to electrify hearts. Nothing. *Alguien salve a la monjita,* someone yells. I wish someone *would* save this little nun, until I see Margarita: her cheeks flushed, her black hair brilliant, dancing between the rows like the most beautiful fool I've ever seen. My legs can no longer hold my weight, and my knees buckle. Everything goes black.

Watermelon Sun

Margarita's feet
dangle as she sits

inside a flamingo
float tickling a sea

of blue marbles. *How
was Sixth Sense?* she

asks. *Cartoons, chick-
flicks and documentaries*

*are a thing here. So is
playing Clue, lotería*

*and restaurant. We order
whatever we want and poof!*

it appears, she says. *We
who?* I ask. *Ciudad Juárez*

*girls. From 1 to 99. The 99ers,
though, they're obsessed*

with hide-and-seek. Ugh,
she says. *I also spy on Cecy,*

*Brenda, my parents. Who-
ever I love,* she says. *Héctor*

too? I ask. *I only liked
him, but I can touch*

his face if I want.
It's made of clay

and clouds, but still,
she says. *I'm sorry,* I

say. *Why? He speaks*
less this way, she says.

I watch Anamaria TV
often, though. Could

you promise me
something? she asks,

holding out her pinky
finger. I give her mine

without knowing what.
Live, she orders, *for me.*

For all of us here.
She smiles, her chin

dimple the last thing I
see before she paddles

away to a sandía sun.

A Slice of Thirty

The beeping of the rising
and falling green line

of my heart wakes me up.
The hospital is cold.

My tongue commands
water, food but my arms

are wired to an IV.
I see Chachita sleeping,

folded into herself.
A new wrinkle cuts

her brow. I want
to say *Mami, I saw*

Margarita. She plays—
she touches—she says—

but my eyes are lead
curtains held up by a silk

thread. I see a slice
of Thirty walking to me

before my brain
gives in to sleep.

A Different Vent Hums

A choir of thoughts resonates in my head: *Still in the hospital. Fainting's not for the faint of heart. Hunger, Thirst.* This last one makes me half-open my eyes.

Papiringo	Chachita
¿Hija?	
	Are you awake?
How do you feel?	
	We need to talk.
Sor is in the past.	
	Tuition will go to a better school.
To a school that's more human.	
	Maybe we can find someone who can help you in a way we can't?
¿Alguien como... un loquero?	
	Maybe a shrink, yes.
Hija, we love you.	
	As you are. But ever since you were a baby you've been a little adult. Please slow down. Life is too short.
Life is precious.	
	And you are precious to us. Remember, we love you. So much.
¿Hija?	
	I think she fell back asleep.
Oh.	
	I wonder where she goes when she sleeps.

I wonder if she knows
that she's my beautiful girl.

                              I think we should just ask.
                              Let her talk.

The vent's soothing hums lose to a lullaby
every daughter wants to hear. I fall fast asleep.

Priscila Calls Me

I read the doctor's orders on my nightstand: "rest." Chachita had to be behind that. *¡Teléfono, Anamaria!* Papiringo calls. Priscila's *hola* is louder than normal. Five seconds go by. Trays hit trays. I think she's in one of her parents' bakeries. *I'm sorry Margarita is not here. How are you feeling?* she says. The bang-bang goes on. *Hey, your Periodic Table cake was delicious,* I say. *Really? It melted, but thanks,* she says. *Priscila? Thank you for being Pipina's friend when I was not, and for defending me that one time,* I say. Five more seconds blush by, the trays stop their banging. Somehow I hear her smile. *De nada,* she says. *Have you heard about jackrabbits and God?* I start, hungry for a new friend.

Situation

Entering Sor, it feels smaller than before. Like
      a cold bodega with nothing to store. I
only hear a faint cricketing, perhaps because
      I sleep better now. I am definitely more
alive than the principal's fake ficus. *Come in,*
      I hear her call. *So, you leave us, Ms.*
Aragón Sosa. What a waste, she says, wasting
      no time. *You had great potential, just*
like her—Ms. Dospasos Sol. Margarita. She
      was—lovely. She clears her throat.
She can't hold my gaze. Her falling façade
      makes me think of Alexa. Of girls who
hide under anger or lip gloss. *Wherever you*
      go next, I wish you luck, she says.
A prefect barges in, her face a spooked horse:
      Ma'am, we have a...situation. ⁻

She Wants to Fly

I tap my feet on the tile while Principal
Martinez goes to resolve "the situation."

Something comes over me. I am not part
of Sor anymore: its mute clapping, its brick

wallpaper or honor-by-grades race. I rub
my chest to soothe the loss, but I feel this

too: excitement. What will it be like to be
someone else five days a week? Who will

I be then? A pat on my shoulders startles me.
The horse-faced prefect says *Come, you may*

be of help because of your...incident. I
stare, clueless, and wait for her to explain.

She just grabs me by the arm like a hitch,
and we sprint through the yard until we

reach the stairs, which we climb in two's.
A cold draft dries my sweat, and before I

can catch my breath, I know our destination:
the gap. I see Principal Martinez first, whose

arm points to the back of a head of blond
hair. Dirt and cement eddy around the pair

of feet: one rooted to the floor, one half
of the other rooted in air, as if testing

the weather. *Alexa?* I call. Nothing. *Alexa?*
I repeat. The hole I felt in my chest minutes

ago has turned into an ant's nest. *No one
can stop me*, she says without facing me.

Alexa, look at me, I beg louder than I plan to.
Her neck creaks. I only see her wet profile.

*Just leave, Anamaria. I'm tired of fighting
to be loved. Sorry for everything,* she says.

I have to do more, so I say, *What if
we jump together?* as I take small steps

towards her. *Why would you do that? I
deserve to be gone. More than Margarita.*

More than any girl in this city! Alexa starts
sobbing, so I run to her, ignoring the wind

moving the hem of her uniform and my pants.
I hold her hand. *Listen.* No girl *deserves this.*

*Let's live to honor Margarita and every girl
we've lost,* I say. Alexa's eyes face me at last.

Tic Tic Two

Tic tic, my window groans, but no more than
      I do. The clock says noon, but I feel cotton
balls behind my eyes. *Tic tic*. I rub my temples
      as I make my way to the light coming
through the curtains. It's Thirty. It's a weekday:
      Chachita or Papiringo could be here. She
taps her left wrist, pressuring me to move. I am
      not in the mood: after Alexa and I walked
away whole from the gap, we took a loud ride
      in an ambulance to an emergency room
where a nurse fed us Dum Dums while we waited
      for the doctor. He asked Alexa, *Do you feel
better now?* without listening, or, just not as hard as
      he listened to her heart. Alexa just nodded.
Then he sent us home. Alexa seemed OK, but I
      wondered all night how OK and for how
long—*tic tic*. Thirty turns an invisible knob, her
      eyes bulging. *Later,* I mouth. She pats
her jeans. She pats her messy abuelita bun.
      A pen comes out of the hairy hive. She
writes on her palm, then presses it to the glass:
      Mr. Yeyé's taking care of you. Open up.

Kaleidoscope

Mr. Yeyé whistles an odd tune in a kitchen covered in confectioner's sugar. Thirty's knock comes. *Hola*, I say to Thirty, and motion her to my room, where I dive into the bed, face first.

Thirty: How are you?
Me: A—xa j—d.

Thirty: I can't understand with your face jammed into the mattress.
Me: Alexa jumped.

Thirty: *What?*
Me: Wait, sorry. She *wanted* to jump. But she didn't. She's OK.

Thirty: What happened?
Me: I said something to stop her. I had to.

Thirty: What did you say?
Me: I just told her to live to honor the girls who've died.

Thirty: That's beautiful. I wish someone had said that to me.
Me: What do you mean?

Thirty: I actually jumped.
Me: Is that why you limp? I don't believe it!

Thirty: Sometimes I don't believe it myself, but yes. [she touches my knee]
Me: [I put my hand on top of hers]

My room turns into a giant kaleidoscope.

In the Gap, In Thirty's Time

The wind whistles *stopjump*
stopjump. She's alone, though
her head throbs with images
of Margarita in a grave full
of flowering cacti. Dust
from Sor's cement floor
trails her jumping feet. No
hands hold her on her way
down. Thoughts are bodi-
less, except Margarita as
a winged girl who says
no. I only feel a ghost of
the pain of her broken
right knee, but it's terrible.
A headache comes in black
waves. Regret comes in
words: *SunAirWaterFood*
ChachitaPapiringoPipina
MargaritaMr.YeyéPoetry
WordsScienceCiudadJuárez
LoveLife. Rings of light
come and go as she opens
her heavy eyes. She cries.
She whispers, *I am alive.*
I am alive. I am alive. I am.

In My Room, In My Time

Me: [I gasp]
Thirty: [she gasps]

Me: That was horrible! *Why* did you jump?
Thirty: A sadness with claws. In me, for me, for Margarita.

Me: A sadness that won't let go? I think I feel that too.
Thirty: Then you need to say, *Papis. I need help. I'm depressed.*

Me: Is "depressed" poet for how we feel?
Thirty: It's just "official." Adults need to put official names to things sometimes.

Me: Why didn't you talk to Chachita and Papiringo when you were thirteen?
Thirty: I was too scared. But you're braver than me. I guess we are not exactly the same.

Me: Why didn't you tell me everything from the beginning?
Thirty: I think *I* was the one who wasn't ready. Losing Margarita broke me, and I just didn't know how to tell you everything without scaring you more. I'm sorry.

Me: I know you really tried to save her, but—
Thirty: I'm so sorry. I—

Me: *But* you saved me.
Thirty: [tears cloud her eyes]

Me: I didn't jump. I'll never jump.
Thirty: Promise? [her voice shakes]

Me: I swear on La Virgen, Jesús and Juan Gabriel.
Thirty: Because you love *you*?

Me: I'm still not sure what that means, but I love you.
Thirty: Me? Really? Why?

Me: You're smart. You're fearless. Your poem wasn't half bad. And you're beautiful.
Thirty: Um...thank you.

Me: De nada.
Thirty: You're also smart and beautiful and—

Me: ¡No, por favor!
Thirty: What does Chachita always say about compliments?

Me: Just say *gracias.*
Thirty: And what did I say about grades?

Me: I am *not* them, I am...I am...I forgot. It's something corny.
Thirty: You are the love—

Me: I give and receive, right! And *I* say...
Thirty: What?

Me: If you're me, and I'm you, then loving you means loving me!
Thirty: Come again?

Me: Thirty talks weird love, but I can't?
Thirty: OK, you win!

Me: Finally! Wait here. I need to use the bathroom.
Thirty: I'll be here...¡niña bonita!

Me: Gracias, gracias. [I take a bow]

What Loving You Is

I flush red and yellow rivulets
down the toilet, get a Kotex

and wash my hands. I look
at my sad eyes, mustache

and soft belly in the mirror:
beautiful in their own way.

But what about what I can't
see? Muscles, bones, cells

and tiny machines that make
my body go. Things, a million

things, could have gone wrong,
starting with the sperm and egg

that made me. What if this pair
failed to meet? I wouldn't be me.

Wait...I just wouldn't *be*. Yet
here I am: the back of my head

still lovely, my brain still fighting
against a clawed sadness. But...

I am...And I have so much
because I exist, just like Thirty

thought about when she jumped.
Her fear of losing life in the blink

of an eye ran deep and electric from
the top of her head to the very tip

of her pinky toes. Wait...Does
loving you mean loving that

you're alive, flaws and all? Can
it be *that* simple? It's even...

corny. I really don't like all these
dot-dot-dots! But if I'm right, why

didn't Thirty just say so? Wait!
I bet *she* doesn't even know!

Is wanting to be the honor roll
queen of loving you, and beating

Thirty at her weird talk a sign
of my old ways? Maybe, but...

I don't care! I splash water on
my face to sharpen my tongue

before going back to her to gloat,
I know what loving you is, do you?

I Went Looking for Her

Outside the house. Maybe I
took too long in the bathroom.
Maybe lime-wrapped pads
are the blood magic that brought
her here. Maybe. But Thirty
is gone. Only a strand of her
hair remains. I waited all day
for her *Meet me at the concession
stand* even though I was not
in Multicinemas. I waited all
night. In the kitchen, I drank
milk and thought of *her*: future
me, but also not exactly me. I
knew things she didn't when she
was thirteen because she told
me, she showed me, so my life
would be different. Better. It
already was: I didn't jump like
she did. But I had been lucky.
No girl should wait for her own
Thirty to arrive. She might not
come. I think about Pipina,
Priscila and Alexa. I think
about how to talk Thirty's
weird love to them without
being *that* weird. Buenas
noches, Thirty. Good night.

Help!

My throat tingles. Words feel easy
until you say them. Choosing when

and where is also a headache. Thirty
didn't prepare me for that. In the end,

it happened in the car, in the morning,
at a red light on Adolfo López Mateos

street on our way back to El Colorín
after visiting new schools, and deciding

on none. Little boys offered to clean
our windshield, Tarahumara abuelitas

asked for Corima in their flowered
skirts, *El Diario* newspaper men showed

the latest found girl on the front page.
A normal day in Ciudad Juárez until

I saw a see-through, iridescent Margarita
playing hide-and-seek around the fuming

cars. Her apple cheeks were neon pink,
alive, even though I knew she wasn't. But

I was. *Muy alive.* So I spit it quick, like gum:
I'm depressed. I need help. Don't be scared.

A Different Love

Mr. Yeyé is making simones when I walk into his coffee shop. My nose takes in the icing and cinnamon rolled into one. He asks how my first shrink appointment went. *It was OK. All we did was talk,* I say. He says he's glad someone will help me feel better. I already do, but not about Ciudad Juárez. *Do you hate our city for taking your niece, Mr. Yeyé?* I ask. His hands stop spiraling dough. *Someone took her, not Ciudad Juárez, and hate does nothing for girls who we will always love,* he says. I never thought about it like that. *Do you love Ciudad Juárez then?* I ask. He said he always would, wouldn't I? *Yes,* I say, but think this: my love for Ciudad Juárez is now more earth than flower. More woman than girl.

13 = 30

13=30   30

found me

handed me

a Kotex   time

love

13   is

lucky

13

13=30

Girl Woman Art

Knock. I look up from my 13 = 30 shape
and Sharpied poem. Pipina, Priscila and

Alexa come in like three teenage girl
musketeers. *Another poem?* Alexa says,

looking at the open page. *Yes. In fact,*
I love poetry as much as I do science,

I confess, half-red. *Cool,* Alexa says.
Since when? Pipina asks. *I like stories*

and math better, Priscila says. *You don't*
think poetry is cursi? I ask, looking down.

No, why? Plus, it's your art, Pipina starts.
Mine is drawing, Priscila's her numbers,

*and Alexa's...*Pipina stumbles. Our eyeballs
look for answers everywhere but on Alexa's

pixie face. She says, *You don't really know*
*me yet, but my art is...*She can't or won't fill

the blank. *Dillard's?* Pipina, Priscila and I
say at the same time. A minute goes by, then

Alexa bursts into laughter. This makes us fall,
like dominoes, in her unexpected lightness.

Oh no, I think I peed myself! Pipina says,
choked with tears. Our own bladders are

sent to the edge, but we can't stop, even
after a chorus of *¡Ya! Enough! I'll stop*

if you stop! Joke fit done, I ask Alexa what
is her art. *Seriously? It's reading. I read*

without being told to. I read everything. I
think my art is also make-up and hair. Is

that stupid? Alexa asks. *No!* I say. *You*
know? Someone told me to let my curls

be free. Help me? I ask. *Yes, please!* Alexa
says, cracking her knuckles. *Is this a love*

letter? Priscila asks, pointing at a note I
hadn't seen before. Thirty must've dropped

it when she disappeared. *Maybe,* I say.
Their *Oooos, Noooos, Guaus* light up

my room, a place in my chest still tender
from losing Margarita, and a word: Niña.

Girl. She is human. She is also art,
and the rib of someone bubbling below

her own skin, fearless: a woman.

Dear Niña Bonita,

13 was just the start of a weird beautiful for me. Here's a glimpse:

AT 15: I had a beautiful quinceañera. I sweated cats and dogs through the tulle and beads of my dress dancing all night. I woke up sore feeling like it was a fever dream. It wasn't, and I wish I had enjoyed it more. Before that: I should've helped Chachita ice those small cakes she put on each table. Forced Papiringo to dance with me more. Chosen a real friend for a chambelán, my main dance partner. Better yet, I shouldn't have had one at all! What if instead of saving money for this party, we had traveled together to Southern México? México is a jewel of asphalt, desert, jungla and beach that I waited too long to see.

AT 18: Boobs, hips, stretch marks, shaving felt like a punishment for being a woman. Some of my friends had curves. Some were wafer-thin. Some of them were in between. The mirror reduced me to big-boned, panzona, stick-legged with no butt to speak of. No concrete category, alone. But I wasn't: all of us were freaked out about our neon-sign of a female body. This shell that hides our truest selves. I should've listened to women around me more. *What do you want? How do you hurt? How can I help?* Worked towards a common goal: to elevate one another, just like ants do when reaching for the sky.

AT 20-24: Love. It's all honey and heat until someone plays marbles with hearts. Until someone rejects you. Why? I asked. I had said "I love you," tutored them in chemistry and baked cakes. In return I got silence, smirks or the dust left after they ran. I became a year-round Grinch who only loved handsome, unreachable pixels like Brad Pitt. Then I saw a little boy fall. He was told "don't cry, get up." I recognized this boy inside the men I had loved. I decided to become a happy hermit. Then I saw Paul: the boy inside him had cried until his heart overflowed.

AT 25-29: Adult acne and this earth-shattering realization after I left medicine: Chachita didn't have a direct line to God. Papiringo couldn't fix all broken things. Chachita and Papiringo were just...human. All these years: had they fed me lies with a glass of milk to wash them down? Depression was splitting me in two: why pull the curtain now? Where were my perfect saviors? The answer came in bits and pieces until I saw it whole: nowhere. They had never been all powerful and all knowing. No parent is. I loved them all the more for it: their humanity gave them the courage to raise and love me. Their humanity made them my Amanda, my Carlos.

AT 30: My body is what it is: a well-oiled machine that takes me places, needs prunes, and dances with some style (A secret: it's all in your face, not your limbs). My brain is what it is too: a muscle that spasms when I don't stop to smell the wet earth. My mother's skinny hands. My father's carne asada. Paul's hair. That is what makes happiness, not grades or accolades. But there are days I feel 13 all over again: I eat my feelings and obsess over work. I sweat sadness. But it stops, it does: whatever is bringing me down is not the end of the world. I am not alone. I write, read and teach. I breathe proud before facing the day's first rays of light.

Love,
Thirty

Notes from the Author

Since the 1990s girls and women have disappeared and been "found" by the hundreds in Ciudad Juárez. The thousands. This book says, *We will always remember you. Your deaths mean more than a headline. Justice is yet to be done.*

Thirty Talks Weird Love is foremost dedicated to the girls and women of Ciudad Juárez whom we've lost. As a Mexican American woman who is a native of Ciudad Juárez, and who walks its streets with a mixture of love, fear, and awe, their loss strikes a nerve frayed in me since I was ten years old. Beyond country and gender, this is my responsibility: to remember and bear witness.

The families of these girls and women don't rest. Their lives are defined by their fight: in protests, in repainting black crosses against pink backgrounds. In living with the memories of their daughters day after day. This book is dedicated to them too: I am awed and humbled by your strength. Your daughters inspire a brand of courage I can only wear with my head bowed through my work as a writer and teacher.

This book is also dedicated to Ciudad Juárez: you will always be my home, mi segunda madre.

***

I've been living in El Paso, Texas for 13 years, but I was born and raised in Ciudad Juárez, México, and my life is not what I pictured it would be when I was 13: I was to be a doctor, not a writer and teacher. This childhood plan stemmed from wanting to soothe the burning backs of my parents, who have worked hard since I can remember. Did they ask for this? Never. This was just my idea of honoring my parents' labor. I also loved science, school, and the prospect of helping babies come into the world. My plans, motivations, and personality were a match.

Fast forward to age 25 when I started medical school in Galveston, Texas. Drinking water from a fire hose is a popular metaphor to describe the kind of learning that goes on during med school. One year into my degree I knew it was inaccurate: it was more like drinking from a roaring waterfall. Nevertheless, I passed my classes and signed up for a Global Medicine track that took me to India for a month during my first summer break. I was changed by that trip. Back from this land of technicolor—from the saris and the food to the energy of its people and its passionate, polyglot health practitioners—I did a preceptorship with Texas Tech's Department of Family Medicine in El Paso. Life was beyond good. I was ready to begin my second year.

Or so I thought. The worst depressive episode of my life surprised me only weeks into the year when I stopped attending class and studied very little. I turned to junk food, Netflix, and drinking water straight from one-gallon containers, which cluttered the floor of my small bedroom. I bathed sporadically. What had happened?

Fast forwards can hide important events. When I was 17, I tried to commit suicide. I never took time to take stock of why. Like Anamaria, I was a nervous and obsessive child who only thought about school and perfection. It makes sense that, when I attempted to take my life, I thought I didn't have the time to talk to my parents and ask for help. What for? I had too many things to do. Too much to learn. Success would justify and bury it all.

Still in Galveston, my daytime existence and diet—Little Debbie Oatmeal Creme Pies, episode after episode of *30 Rock*, and water—was further complicated by dreams of a gun pointed at my temple. I recognized the feeling from when I was 17: I wanted relief. Again. Success had come up short. This time I talked a little to my roommate and best friend, Jazmín, about my "lack of motivation." She helped as much as she could with the information she had, but to no avail. I couldn't go back to that driven self that I had been.

The pushing force arrived through a thought I had when lying on the floor, which I did often to anchor my head to the ground: *what would Leyla, my niece who was only a few months old, be told about me if I died?* This opened a floodgate: *Will she be happy? What will she grow up to be like? What will she look like?* I couldn't bear not to know.

I made an appointment to speak to a nurse practitioner about my symptoms. I was prescribed an antidepressant. I left Galveston for El Paso with plans to come back after a one-year leave of absence. During that time, I took care of Leyla while my sister worked, and lived by my niece's daytime feeding and napping schedule. It was a steep learning curve, but I was thankful because watching her grow occupied most of my time. There was also Paul, and knowing that kind of love and support for the first time. As far as therapy, I visited a psychologist once or twice to talk about what had happened, but I was still hyper focused on the future: I would pull through and laugh about it all when I graduated, when I got my first paycheck.

Once back in Galveston, I changed my studying methods, exercised, continued taking my antidepressant, and visited a psychiatrist when I started losing sleep over the things I hadn't done to "master" the material. She prescribed medication for that and told me I would be able to rest after my study marathons. I didn't. Then I took my first exam: I knew I had failed it even before I saw my grade.

My brain went into shock, and the meaning of this failure became worse than the reality. So, days before my 27th birthday, I emailed my dean to say I was leaving and sold my books and furniture on Facebook to raise the money for a small U-Haul. First-year medical students who came over to pick up their purchases were often puzzled when they asked if I had graduated, and I replied no. Yes, I wanted to say, I was leaving all of it behind: my childhood plans, my way to honor my parents.

Eight years have gone by since this happened. I have no regrets because I acted in self-defense for probably the first time in my school-obsessed life. I've come to realize that this so-called "failure" was only a setback. Evidently my illness was not under control; otherwise, I think I would've accepted that grade for what it was: a pebble, not a boulder. Over time, the pebble I skipped led me to two callings I deeply cherish: writing and teaching. And both have allowed me to explore bigger questions: what if I had talked to a therapist when I was 17? What if that student were to seek help? Should I step in to help them consider or accelerate this decision?

As some of my former high-school and college students will attest, the answer is often yes. First through informal conversations—during recess, tutoring sessions, office hours, after class, in emails—when students shared their experiences and I shared mine. Then through Thirty, and now *Thirty Talks Weird Love*. At first, my desire to share what I had learned in hindsight with the young people I was working with was stronger than the memories of my teenagehood, or lack thereof, through Anamaria. But she came into the picture, vital and refreshing, just as my students do, to teach me that in looking to our past we should see just how strong and beautiful we were.

As far as the present, it's all we have. A cliché, I realize, but we are here now. Not yesterday or tomorrow. So, don't wait: get to the phone or computer and find the help you need to make this time on earth as joyful and full as it can be (suicidepreventionlifeline.org). Not ready? Go to family, friends, or teachers who talk about mental illness openly; they might help you get over the threshold. Go to books that do the same. Authors manage mental illness awareness in their work in different ways, but I believe most of us are just trying to say this: *Dear Reader, you are not alone.* As for *Thirty Talks Weird Love*, I want to say there's both an Anamaria and a Thirty within you waiting to be heard. Please end the wait, and listen to them.

Acknowledgements

To the Cinco Puntos Press family. Lee Byrd, my editor extraordinaire: Thank you for taking a risk. Thank you for putting up with my growing pains and long notes. Thank you for being a champion of writers of color and their stories. Thank you, thank you, thank you. This book wouldn't be without you. Stephanie Frescas Macías: Thank you for being an unwavering source of support, patience and kindness, and for your detail-oriented, keen mind. The future of book publishing and editing is safe in your hands. Zeke Peña: Thank you for your design magic, for giving shape to this book with so much patience and devotion. Mary Fountaine: Thank you for your beautiful voice; every time I picked up the phone or went to Cinco and was welcomed by you, I felt at ease. Bobby and John Byrd: Thank you for loving women and their work, and for supporting their dreams.

To Paulina Magos: Thank you for your art. *Thirty Talks Weird Love* started to breathe with your cover illustration.

To Leyla, my lovely niece, and the closest thing I have to a daughter. When I first held you in my arms, I fell in love. Now that you're eight going on nine, you inspire me with your paintings, your brain, your kindness, and those brown eyes that threaten to fly away with those long, long eyelashes.

To Yazmín, my sister, you are beautiful and brilliant. Your sense of humor (you were the one who told me the balloon-in-a desert joke) saved my life so many times, even though I didn't know it when we were younger. Your dedication to your art and teaching pushes me to fight.

To mi mami, Amanda, the real Chachita: it took me so long to love you right. I'm still learning, actually. But I've always seen what a strong, stunning woman you are. You are a force of nature. Thank you for everything you've done for me: writing beautiful letters, explaining money, teaching me how to make food (lentejas, albóndigas, etc.), driving me across the border for reasons big and small. My courage and idea of what love is comes from you.

To mi papi, Carlos, the real Papiringo: it's taken me too long to love you right too. Tu eres mi canario, mi piedra. El hombre al que siempre puedo llamar cuando sufro, cuando necesito una mano, una charla, un abrazo. Gracias. I remember how you patiently explained math to me through high school. You still explain so many things to me, including love, gardening, and Mexican politics. My sad eyes, my calves, and my strength come from you.

To both of you: thank you for loving your machetera, flawed daughter just as she is.

To Paul, ageless pan dulce of a man: I wish I had received Thirty's letter when I was thirteen. I would've wasted less time. But truth is, I wouldn't have believed you existed. You are a true dream. You're sweetness and generosity inside a marvelous physical exterior. Your jet-black hair is a piece of night sky I've craved since I met you, and I can't stop looking at your eyes as you patiently correct my grammar and read my words with all of your heart. This book was born from your unconditional love for my brain, my womanhood, and my craving for weird food. This book will always be ours.

To my parents and uncle-in-law: Luz, Ken, and Douglas.

You've been counselors, publicists, cheerleaders. A second family. You've raised a wonderful man I have the privilege to love and be loved by. Especially to Luz: You've loved me as a daughter. You've lent me your ear so many times and encouraged me to talk to you as a friend about my life, including my struggles with depression. Thank you. To John and Michael, thank you for your brotherhood.

To Kito, my cousin, the brother I never had: thank you for your nerdiness, for always loving my parents, for your joking around (even at my expense!) so I could laugh, and be young for once. Gracias por querer a la Aletis, tu prima la seria, la del mal carácter, pero la que siempre te ha querido con todo su corazón.

To Richie, my cousin, the second brother I never had: thank you for your love, dulzura and your unconditional faith in me since I was a grumpy girl always glued to the kitchen table doing homework. Eres un "amor con patas", un corazón andando, siempre dispuesto a darme a mí y a mis papás más, más y más. Te adoro, mi hermoso primo y hermano.

To my friends, old and new. Thank you for accepting me as I am at different stages of my life: Sybil Acosta, Edgar Aguilar Araoz, Antonio Baca, Francisco Barraza, Regina Bustillos, Priscila Castillo, Héctor Cisneros, Paula Cucurella, Mandy Campos, Raúl "Pato" Carrillo, Andie Castillo, David Cruz, Alejandra Diaz, Sarah Demers, Tania & Omar Félix, Gloria Fogerson, Jazmín Gonzalez, Jeanette Hernandez, Saúl Hernández, Victor & Maira Jackson, Camille Johnson, David Kosturakis, Alejandra "Pipina" Licón, Andrew T. Nelson, Irma Nikicicz, Emily Martinez, Suzie Masoud, Mireya Perez, Gustavo Ortega, Rachel Quintana, Karla Reyes Almodóvar,

Claudia Rodriguez, Carmen Rubio, Sandy Salinas, Criseida Santos Guevara, Maria Torres, Carmen Vargas, Emmanuel & Karen Villalobos, Stella Winters, Liz Zubiate, Oscar Zapata.

To my students. Thank you for inspiring me to be braver. Because of you I have become a better person and writer. Thank you sharing your writing and life with me. This is for you: André Aguilar, Aaron Alcazar, Maria & Yeraldin Aragon, Daisy Arciniega, Dasseny Arreola, Gabrielle Barrientos, Carson Bennett, Itzel Bermudez, Travis Bevis, Louie Carlos, Katie Clanan, Melissa Coronado, Ruby De Anda, Katherine Espinoza, Jazmin Flores, Paloma Gallego, Lizbeth Garcia, Yaritza Garcia, Magaly Guardian, Karla Hernandez, Andrea Herrera Aguirre, Dylan Hall, Christian Hernandez, Ileana & Karyme Hernandez, Carolina Jacquez, Samantha Lechuga, Marissa Lerma, Aida Licón, Ingrid Lopez, Jazmin Martinez Acosta, Lydia Mendoza, Joseline Millan, Dafne Mota, Olivia Mueller, Elisa Moton, Ivan Parra, Cinthia Ponce, Celeste Reyes, Daniela Rosales, Lina & Adolfo Ruiz, Kimberly Saenz, Paulina Spencer, Kera Steele, Antonia Taylor, America Torres, Jose Vasquez Benitez, Naomi Valenzuela, Eddie Velazquez, Aylin Vejar. To the Canutillo poetry girls. I miss you; you're a breath of fresh air: Alex, Alexis, Brianna, Chastelyn, Daelyn, Jocelyn, Lizzete, Talya.

To my teachers and mentors, thank you dearly for your patience with my long emails and slow-learning ways. Rosa Alcalá (You taught me poetry for the first time, you read and replied to my Galveston emails, you believed in me and this book from the beginning, and no gracias will ever be enough), Nelson Cardenas, Andrea Cote Botero (Your generosity is uncommon; I still pinch myself to remind myself you're this real, this talented, this hermosa), Daniel

Chacón (You've said "teach!", you've said "can I help?", you've said "chill" when I need it and for that ¡mil gracias!), José de Piérola, Michelle Guzmán Armijo, Tim Z. Hernandez (You've taken calls, answered countless questions, and made me realize that ¡sí, señor! here we are, Latinx and proud), Maryse Jayasuriya, Jorge López Austin (Rest in science teacher's paradise), Charmaine Martin, Katja Michael, Sasha Pimentel (You helped me find my voice and said "sister" when I felt the loneliest; you said write, write, write), Luis Arturo Ramos, Cristina Rivera Garza, Lauren Rosenberg, David Ruiter (You've been on my team since 2005, a friend and mentor who's taught me to face hard truths and keep my head high; there's no comparison for thee), Benjamin Alire Sáenz, Jeffrey Sirkin, Oscar Troncoso, Sergio Troncoso, Lex Williford, Sylvia Zéleny (You answer every text, you say "así está la cosa, Ale," and I fight to write another day).

And to my indirect teachers and mentors, thank you for your work, your books: Elizabeth Acevedo, Gloria Anzaldúa, Fatimah Asghar, Margaret Atwood, Donald Barthelme, Jericho Brown, Sandra Cisneros, Tarfia Faizullah, Gabriel García Márquez, Demetria Martinez, Juan Felipe Herrera, Barbara Kingsolver, Toni Morrison, Valeria Luiselli, Isabel Quintero, Sharon Olds, Joyce Carol Oates, José Olivarez, Sigrid Nunez, Karen Russell, Erika L. Sánchez, J.D. Salinger, Patricia Smith, Evie Shockley, Jacqueline Woodson.